There was absolutely no reason to feel a jolt, electrifying or otherwise. And yet, there it was.

Jolting. Electrifying. Fleeting, granted, but still very much there. Completely unexpected, it zipped along the skin of her arms and simultaneously swirled up along the back of her neck.

Janice caught her breath, trying to make her pulse slow down. She did her best to appear unaffected, as if, for a moment, her insides hadn't just turned to jelly.

"Thanks." Straightening, she picked up the contracts—one for each room—and placed them on the table. "Let's go over these, shall we? I don't want you finding that you're in for any surprises."

Too late, he thought. Because his reaction to her had already more than surprised him.

Dear Reader,

In my town, there's one residential development that has taken three separate homes and fashioned them to look like one large, beautiful estate. When I was a kid, my mother dreamed about buying a duplex so that I would be right there, and I remember thinking that, although I dearly loved my mother, the thought of living in a duplex made me feel claustrophobic—until I saw these homes.

I still drive by the same area to look at the houses and imagine living there. And so THE SONS OF LILY MOREAU was born. Three very different men with three very different fathers and one larger-than-life mother. In the book you're holding, you have Philippe's story. Philippe is the oldest of the three and, perforce, the glue that holds them all together. But despite his patriarchal tendencies, Philippe doesn't think that marriage is in the cards for him. You can't find what you don't have time to look for—or can you? Come find out.

As always, I thank you for reading and I wish you love,

Marie Ferrarella

MARIE FERRARELLA

REMODELING THE BACHELOR

SPECIAL EDITION

Published by Silhouette Books

America's Publisher of Contemporary Romance

SILHOUETTE BOOKS

ISBN-13: 978-0-373-24845-2
ISBN-10:   0-373-24845-8

REMODELING THE BACHELOR

Copyright © 2007 by Marie Rydzynski-Ferrarella

Selected Books by Marie Ferrarella

Silhouette Special Edition

Her Good Fortune #1665
Because a Husband Is Forever #1671
The Measure of a Man #1706
She's Having a Baby #1713
Her Special Charm #1726
Husbands and Other Strangers #1736
The Prodigal M.D. Returns #1775
Mother in Training #1785
Remodeling the Bachelor #1845

Silhouette Romantic Suspense

In Broad Daylight #1315
Alone in the Dark #1327
Dangerous Disguise #1339
The Heart of a Ruler #1412
The Woman Who Wasn't There #1415
Cavanaugh Witch #1431
Her Lawman on Call #1451
Diagnosis: Danger #1460
My Spy #1472

Harlequin Next

Starting from Scratch #17
Finding Home #45
The Second Time Around #73

MARIE FERRARELLA

This *USA TODAY* bestselling and RITA® Award-winning author has written over one hundred and fifty novels for Silhouette Books, some under the name Marie Nicole. Her romances are beloved by fans worldwide. Visit her Web site at www.marieferrarella.com.

To Helen Conrad, my bridge over troubled waters.
Thank you.

Chapter One

"When are you going to get that cracked sink fixed?" Beau de la Croix asked good-naturedly as he slid back into his place at the poker table.

The question was addressed to Philippe Zabelle, his cousin and the host of their weekly poker game. Beau and several other friends and relatives showed up here at Philippe's to talk, eat and bet toothpicks on the whimsical turn of the cards. They used colored toothpicks instead of chips or money because those were the house rules and Philippe, easygoing about so many things, was very strict about that.

Philippe's dark eyebrows rose slightly above his light

green eyes at the innocent but still irritating query. Beau had hit a sore spot. Everyone at the circular table was aware of that.

"When I get around to it," Philippe replied evenly.

"Better hope that's not soon," Georges Armand, Philippe's half brother commented, battling the grin that begged to break out across his tanned face. "If Philippe puts his hand to it, that's the end of the sink."

Philippe, the oldest of famed artist Lily Moreau's three sons, shifted his steely gaze toward Georges, his junior by two years. "Are you saying that I'm not handy?"

Alain Dulac, Philippe's other half brother, as blond as Philippe was dark, bent over with laughter at the very idea of his older brother holding an actual tool in his hand. "Oh God, Philippe, you're so far from handy that if *handy* were Los Angeles, you'd be somewhere in the Atlantic Ocean. Drowning," Alain finally managed, holding his sides because they hurt.

Georges discarded two cards and momentarily frowned at the rest of his hand. "Two," he decided out loud, then looked over to his right and Philippe. "Everyone knows you've got lots of talents, Philippe, but being handy is just not one of them."

Philippe tried not to take offense, but it bothered him nonetheless. For the most part, he considered himself a free thinker, a person who believed that no one should be expected to fit into a given slot or pigeonholed because of gender or race. With the flamboyant and outspoken Lily Moreau as his mother, a woman who made the fictional Auntie Mame come off like a cloistered nun, he couldn't help but have an open mind.

Even so, it got under his skin that he barely knew the difference between a Phillips-head screwdriver and a flat-head one. Men were supposed to know these things, it was a given, written in some giant book of man-rules somewhere.

The fact that he not only couldn't rebuild an automobile engine but was pretty stumped if one refused to start, didn't bother him. Lots of men were ignorant about what went on under the hoods of things housed in their garage.

But not being handy around the house, well, that was another story entirely.

Still, he had no natural ability, nor even a fostered one. He'd always been too busy either studying or being both mother and father to his brothers because his mother had once more taken off with a show, or, just as likely, with a man. Growing up, he'd found himself taking on the role of buffer, placing himself between the endless parade of nannies and his two younger brothers. Once out of their rebellious teens, Georges and Alain had both acknowledged that even though they loved their mother dearly, Philippe was the only reason they had turned out normal. Or at least reasonably so.

That didn't stop them from teasing him whenever the opportunity arose. Their affection for the man they considered the head of the family actually seemed to promote it.

"One," Alain requested, throwing down his card first. After glancing at the new addition, he looked up at Philippe. He put on the face that Philippe knew was the undoing of every fluttering female heart at the university Alain was currently attending. A university whose tuition bill found its way into his mailbox twice a year and which he promptly and willingly paid. "Too late to change my mind and get the old one back?"

There wasn't even a hint of humor on Philippe's face. "After insulting me?"

"Wasn't an insult, Philippe," his cousin Remy assured him. Remy, a geologist, was closer to Alain in age than Philippe. "Alain was only telling it the way it is. Hey," he added quickly, forestalling any fallout from the man they all admired, "we all love you, Philippe, but you know you'll never be the first one any of us call if we find that we've got a clogged drain."

"Or a cabinet door that won't close right," Vincent Mirabeau called over from the far side of the kitchen. "Like this one." To illustrate his point, Vincent, another one of Philippe's cousins and Lily's godson, went through elaborate motions to close the closet door. Creaking, it returned to its place, approximately an inch and a half away from its mate, just hanging in midspace. "I think you should bite the bullet and hire someone to remodel this place."

Remy put in his two cents. "Or at least the bathroom and the kitchen."

Philippe folded his hand and placed it face down on the table, his eyes sweeping over his brothers and cousins.

"What's wrong with this place?" he asked.

He'd bought the house with the first money he'd managed to save up after opening up his own software design company. The moment he'd seen it, he'd known that the unique structure was for him. To the passing eye, the house where he received his mail appeared to be a giant estate. It was only when the passing eye stopped passing and moved closer that the perception changed. His house was just one of three houses, carefully designed to look like one. There was one door in the center, leading to his house. Other doors located on either end of the structure opened the other two houses. Thanks to his initial down payment, Georges and Alain lived in those. They all had their privacy but were within shouting distance if a quick family meeting was needed. Because Lily was their mother, the need for one of these was not as rare for them as it was for some families.

"Nothing's wrong with this place," Beau was quick to say. They all knew how attached to the house Philippe was. "At least, nothing a good handyman couldn't fix."

Philippe's expression remained uncharacteristically stony. "C'mon, Philippe," Remy urged, "every time you turn on the faucet in the kitchen, it sounds like you're listening to the first five bars of 'When the Saints Come Marching In.'"

Before Philippe could protest, Remy turned the handle toward the left. Hot water slowly emerged, but a strange echoing rattling noise in the pipes preceded the appearance of any liquid.

Philippe sighed. There was no point in pretending he would get around to fixing that, either. He didn't even know where to start. When it came to the faucet, his ability began and ended with turning the spigots on or off.

Tossing a bright pink toothpick onto the pile of red, blue, green and yellow, Philippe asked, "Anyone else want to bet?"

Vincent shook his head, throwing in his cards. "Too rich for my blood."

"Count me out." Remy followed suit.

But Beau grinned. "I'll see your pink toothpick," he tossed one in, "and raise you a green one."

Picking up a green toothpick from his dwindling pile, Philippe debated. Green represented five cents; he rarely went higher than that on a single bet. His father, Jon Zabelle, had been a charming incurable gambler. The man had single-handedly almost brought them down and was responsible for Lily Moreau's brief and unfortunate flirtation with frightening poverty. That period of time, long in his past and no more than three months in length, had left an indelible mark on Philippe.

It also allowed him to recognize the occasional craving to bet as a potential problem.

Forewarned, Philippe treated any obstacle head on. Since he liked to play cards and he liked to gamble, he made sure that it would never result in his losing anything more a handful of colorful toothpicks. The big loser at his table wound up doing chores to make payment, not going to an ATM machine.

"I call," Philippe announced, tossing in the green toothpick to match his cousin's.

"Three of a kind," Beau told him, spreading out two black nines with a red one in between.

"Me, too," Philippe countered, setting down three fours, one by one. And then he added, "Oh, and I've also got two of a kind." The fours were joined by a pair of queens.

Beau huffed, staring down at the winning hand. "Full house, you damn lucky son of a gun." He pushed the "pot," with its assorted array of toothpicks, toward his oldest cousin.

"Gonna cash in this time and spend all your 'winnings' on renovating the house?" Remy teased as Philippe sorted out the different colors and placed them in their appropriate piles.

Philippe didn't bother looking at his cousin. "I don't have the time to start hunting for a decent contractor."

Vincent's grin went from ear to ear. He stuck his hand into his back pocket and pulled out his wallet.

"Just so happens, I have the name of a contractor right here in my wallet."

Philippe stopped sorting, feeling like a man who'd been set up. "Oh?"

"Yeah. Somebody named J. D. Wyatt," Vincent told him. "Friend of mine had some work done on his place. Said it was fast and the bid was way below anything the other contractors he'd contacted had come through with."

Which could be good, or could be bad, Philippe thought. The contractor could be hungry for work or he could be using sub-grade material. If he decided to hire this J.D., he was going to have to stay on top of him.

Philippe thought for a moment. He knew his brothers and cousins were going to keep on ribbing him until he gave in. In all fairness, he knew the place could stand to have some work done. He just hated the hassle of having someone else do it.

Better that than the hassle of you pretending you know what you're doing and messing up, big time, a small voice in his head whispered.

For better or for worse, he made up his mind. He'd give it a go. After all, he wasn't an unreasonable man and the place did look like it was waiting to get on the disaster-area list.

He could always cancel if it didn't work out. "This J.D. have a phone number where I could reach him?"

Vincent was already ahead of him. "Just so happens,"

he plucked the card out of his wallet and held it out to his cousin, "I've got it right here."

"Serendipity," Remy declared, grinning as Philippe looked at him quizzically. "Can't mess with serendipity."

"Since when?" Philippe snorted.

Remy had an answer for everything. "Since it'll interfere with your karma."

Philippe snorted even louder. He didn't believe in any of that nonsense. That was his mother's domain. Karma, tarot cards, tea leaves, mediums, everything and anything that pretended to link her up with the past. Although he loved the woman dearly and would do anything for her, he'd spent most of his life trying to be as different from his mother as humanly possible—from both his parents.

That was why he'd turned his back on the artistic ability that he'd so obviously inherited. Because he didn't want to go his mother's route.

Lily Moreau had coaxed her first born to pick up a paintbrush in his hand even before she'd encouraged him to pick up a toothbrush and brush his teeth. If he made it as an artist, he could always buy new teeth, she'd informed him cheerfully.

But he had dug in his heels and been extremely stubborn. He refused to draw or paint anything either under her watchful eye or away from it. Only when he was absently killing time, most likely on hold on the phone, did he catch himself doodling some elaborate figure in pencil.

He was always quick to destroy any and all evidence. He was his mother's son, as well as his father's, but there was no earthly reason that he could see to admit to either, at least not when it came to laboring under their shadows.

He wanted to make his own way in the world, be his own person, make his own mistakes and have his own triumphs. And this was one of the reasons it really bothered him that he wasn't up to the task of fixing things in his own place. Neither his father, now dead, nor his mother, alive enough for both of them, could claim to be even remotely handy. If Philippe were handy, he would be even more different from his parents.

But for that to ever happen, he was going to need lessons. Intense lessons. He glanced down at the card in his hand. Maybe this would turn out all right after all.

"Okay," he nodded, tucking the card into the back pocket of his jeans, "I'll call this J.D. when I get a chance."

"Before the bathroom sink breaks in half?" Georges asked.

Philippe nodded. "Before the bathroom sink breaks in half," he promised. He picked up the deck of cards again and looked around. "Now, do you guys want to play poker or do you just want to sit around, complaining about my house?"

"All in favor of complaining about Philippe's house," Georges declared, raising his hand in the air as he looked around the table, "raise your hand."

Every hand around him shot up, but Philippe focused

his attention exclusively on his brother. Grabbing a handful of chips—the crunchy kind—he threw them at Georges. Laughing, Georges responded in kind.

Which was how the poker game devolved into a food fight that lasted until all the remaining edible material—and the toothpicks—and been commandeered and pressed into service.

The result was a huge mess and a great deal of laughter, punctuated by a stream of colorful words that didn't begin to describe what had gone on.

Hours later, after he had gotten them to all lend a hand and clean up, the gathering finally broke up and they all went their separate ways. Alain returned to his law books and Georges declared that he had a late date waiting for him, one that, he'd whispered confidentially, held a great deal of promise. Which only meant that Georges thought he was going to get lucky.

Remy, Vincent and Beau went back to whatever it was that occupied them in their off-hours. Trouble, mostly, Philippe thought fondly. Probably instigated by Henri and Joseph, first cousins and two of the more silent members of the weekly poker game.

It was still early by his old standards. But his old standards hadn't had to cope with deadlines and program bugs that insisted on manifesting themselves despite his diligent attempts to squash them. Program bugs he needed to iron out of his latest software package before he submitted it to Lyon Enterprises, his software publisher. The deadline was breathing down his neck.

He didn't have to work this hard. He *chose* to work this hard. Philippe had made his fortune on a software package that he'd designed five years ago, a package that had become indispensable to the advertising industry. Streamlined and efficient, it was now considered the standard by which all other such programs were measured. There was no need for him to keep hours that would have only gladdened the heart of a Tibetan monk, but, unlike his late father, he had never believed in coasting. He liked being kept busy, liked creating, liked having a schedule to adhere to and something tangible to shoot for every day. He wasn't the idle type.

His mother's second husband, Georges's father, had been a self-made millionaire, owing his fortune to a delicate scent that lured scores of women with far too much money on their hands. André Armand was a man who slept late and partied into the wee hours of the morning. It was because of André that they had the lifestyle they now enjoyed.

Even before André had married his mother, the man had taken to him. The moment the vows were uttered, he'd taken him under his wing, viewing him as a protégé. But Philippe quickly learned that although he really liked the man, the life André led was not one that appealed to him at all, even as an adolescent. It was because of André that Philippe had come to the conclusion that no matter how rich he was, a man needed a purpose.

He'd never forgotten it, nor let either one of his brothers forget it. He'd made sure that his brothers did their lessons and excelled in school, even when they said they didn't need to.

"You need to make a difference in this world," he'd told them over and over again, "no matter how small. Or else all you are is a large mound of dust, just passing through."

As he slipped his hands into his back pockets, the tips of the fingers of his right hand came in contact with what felt like a piece of paper. Drawing it out, Philippe stared for a second before he recalled where he'd gotten it and why.

The contractor.

Right.

Well, if he didn't make the call right now, he knew he wouldn't. Life had a habit of overwhelming him at times, especially whenever his mother was in town and rumor had it Hurricane Lily was due in soon. Details tended to get buried and lost if he didn't attend to them immediately.

Do it now or let it go, Philippe thought with a half smile.

Making his way to the nearest phone, Philippe glanced at his watch to make sure it wasn't too late to call. It was a little before ten. Still early, he thought as he began to tap out the embossed hunter-green numbers on the card.

The phone on the other end rang three times. No one picked up.

Philippe was about to hang up when he heard the receiver suddenly coming to life.

And then, the most melodic voice he'd ever heard proceeded to tell him: "You've reached J. D. Wyatt's office. I'm sorry we missed you call. Please leave your number and a detailed message as to what you want done and we'll get back to you."

Obviously this was either Wyatt's secretary or, more likely, his wife. The sensual sound of her voice planted thoughts in his head and made him want to request having "things done" that had nothing to do with renovating parts of his house and everything to do with renovating parts of him. Or his soul, he silently amended.

He was currently in between encounters. Encounters, not relationships, because they weren't that. Relationships took time, effort, emotional investment; all of which he'd seen come to naught, especially in his mother's life. There'd been some keepers in his mother's lot, most notably Alain's father and a man named Alexander Walters. But as much as his mother loved being in a relationship, loved having a man around, she had always been the restless kind. No matter how good a relationship was, eventually his mother felt the need to leave it, to shed it like a skin she'd outgrown. She'd left all three of her husbands, divorcing them before they'd died. Remained friends with all of the men she'd loved even years after she'd moved on.

His mother couldn't seem to function without a relationship in her life, especially when it was in its birthing stages. She loved being in love. He had never seen the need for that, the need for garnering the pain involved in ending something. He'd never wanted to be in that position, so he wasn't. It was as simple as that.

Feelings couldn't be hurt if they weren't invested—on either side. After a while, it seemed natural to have female company only on the most cursory level. To enjoy an encounter without promising anything beyond tonight and then moving on.

He didn't know any other way.

The beep he heard on the other end of the line roused him, bringing him back from his momentary revelry. "Um, this is Philippe Zabelle." He rattled off his telephone number. "I got your name from a friend of a friend. I need some remodeling work done on two of my bathrooms. I thought you might come by my place at around seven tomorrow night if that's convenient for you." He recited his address slowly. "If I don't get a call from you, I'll be expecting you tomorrow at seven. See you then."

Philippe hung up. He absolutely hated talking to machines, even ones with sexy voices. As he went up the stairs to his bedroom, he thought about how people were far too isolated and dependent on machines to do their work for them.

And then he smiled to himself. It was a rather ironic thought, given the nature of what he did for a living. His smile widened. The world was a strange place.

Chapter Two

The next morning, Philippe hit the ground running.

Usually reliable, his inner alarm clock had decided to go on strike. Instead of six-thirty, the time he normally woke up during the work week, Philippe rolled over and stared in disbelief at the digital clock beside the bed.

Burning in bright, bold red shone the numbers 7:46 a.m.

The second his brain registered the discrepancy between the time he intended to get up and the actual hour, Philippe tumbled out of bed. He then proceeded to race through his shower and decide not to bother shaving. He was down in the kitchen at exactly one minute before eight o'clock.

He would have made himself toast and scrambled eggs if he'd had bread. Or eggs. Instead breakfast consisted of the last of his coffee and a couple of close-to-stale pieces of Swiss cheese, the latter being part of what he'd served last night along with beer, junk food and conversation.

Leaning a hip against the counter as he finished the last of the unexceptional cheese, he shook his head. It was time to surrender and give in to the inevitable: he needed a housekeeper. Someone who stopped by maybe once a week, did the grocery shopping and gave the house a fast once-over. That was all that was really necessary. As the oldest and the one who often was left in charge, Philippe had learned to run a fairly tight, not to mention neat, ship. The only thing in utter disarray was the desk in his home office.

Actually, if he was being honest with himself, most of the office looked that way, what with books left open to pertinent sections and a ton of paper scattered in all four corners of the room, covering most of the available flat surfaces. He supposed, in a way, it was a statement about the way his life operated. His private affairs were neatly organized while his work looked as if he'd recently been entertaining a grade four hurricane on the premises.

Finished eating, Philippe wiped his fingers on the back of his jeans and made his way over to the telephone. Ten minutes later, he'd placed an ad in the local paper as well as on the newspaper's Internet site for an experienced housekeeper to do light housekeeping once a week.

He frowned as he hung up.

Hiring someone to invade his space, even briefly, wasn't a choice he was happy about, but he had to face it. It was a necessary evil. Business was very good and the demand on his time was high. Aside from the weekly poker games, of late he seemed to be spending all of his time working. That left no time for the minor essentials—like the procurement of foodstuff. He needed someone to do that for him.

He could have advertised for an assistant, Philippe thought as he made his way to the back of the house and the organized chaos that was his home office, but that would have meant a big invasion. He knew himself better than that. No, a housekeeper was the better way to go, he decided.

Planting the opened can of flat soda he'd discovered sitting in the back of his all-but-barren refrigerator on the first space he unearthed by his computer, Philippe flipped on the radio that resided on the bookcase beside his desk. Classical music filled the air as he sat down and got to work. Within seconds, he was enmeshed in programming language and completely oblivious to such things as time and space and earthly surroundings.

During the course of the day, when his brain begged for a break and his stomach upbraided him for abuse, Philippe made his way to the kitchen to forage for food. Lunch had consisted of pretzels, made slightly soggy by being left out overnight. Dinner had been more of the same with a handful of assorted nuts downed as a chaser. But the food hardly mattered.

It was his work that was important and it was progressing well. He'd gotten further along on the new software than he'd expected and that always gave him a sense of satisfaction, as did the fact that he handled everything by himself. He created the programs, designed the artwork and developed the tutorial and self-help features, something that was taking on more and more importance with each software package he created.

With a heartfelt sigh, Philippe closed down his computer. Rising to his feet, he went to the kitchen to get himself the last bottle of beer to celebrate a very productive, if exhausting, day.

He had just opened the refrigerator door to see if perhaps he'd missed something edible in his prior forages when he heard the doorbell. Releasing the refrigerator door again, he glanced at his watch. Seven o'clock. Both his brothers and his friends knew that he generally knocked off around seven. One of them had obviously decided to visit.

Good, he could use a little company right about now. Maybe he and whoever was at his door could go out for a bite to eat.

His stomach rumbled again.

Several bites, Philippe amended, striding toward the door.

"Hi," he said cheerfully as he swung open the door.

It took him less than half a second to realize he'd just uttered the greeting to a complete stranger. A very attractive complete stranger wearing a blue pullover sweater and a pair of light-colored faded jeans that adhered in such a way as to drive the stock of jeans everywhere sky-high. The blonde was holding the hand of a little girl who, for all intents and purposes, was an exact miniature of her.

Like the woman whose hand she was holding, the little girl was slight and petite and very, very blond. He guessed that she had to be about five or so, although he was on shaky ground when it came to anything to do with kids.

Philippe looked back to the woman with the heart-shaped face. He had to clear his throat before he asked, "Can I help you?"

Eyes the color of cornflowers in bloom washed over him slowly, as if she was taking his measure. It was then that he remembered he was barefoot and wearing the first T-shirt he'd laid his eyes on this morning, the one that had shrunk in the wash. And that when he worked, he had a habit of running his hands through his hair, making it pretty unruly by the end of the day. That, along with his day-old stubble and worn clothes probably made him look one step removed from a homeless person.

Philippe glanced at the little girl. Rather than look frightened, she was grinning up at him. But the woman holding her hand appeared somewhat skeptical as she continued to regard him. She and the child remained firmly planted on the front step.

He was about to repeat his question when she suddenly answered it—and added to his initial confusion. "I came about the job."

"The job?" he echoed, momentarily lost. And then it hit him. The woman with the perfect mouth and translucent complexion was referring to the housekeeping position he'd called the paper about this morning. Boy, that was fast.

"Oh, the job," he repeated with feeling, glad that was finally cleared up. Beautiful women did not just appear on his doorstep for no reason, not unless they were looking for Georges. "Right. Sure. C'mon in," he invited, gesturing into the house.

Philippe stepped back in order to allow both the woman and the little girl with her to come inside.

The woman still seemed just the slightest bit hesitant. Then, winding her left hand more tightly around her purse, she entered. Her right hand was firmly attached to the little girl. Philippe found himself vaguely curious as to what the woman had in her purse that seemed to give her courage. Mace? A gun? He decided maybe it was better that he didn't know.

"My name's Kelli, what's yours?" The question came not from the woman but from the child, uttered in a strong voice that seemed completely out of harmony with her small body.

He wondered if Kelli would grow into her voice. "Philippe," he told her.

The girl nodded, as if she approved of the name. It amused him that she didn't find his name odd or funny because of the French pronunciation. She had old eyes, he noted.

The personification of curiosity, Kelli scanned her surroundings. Had she not been tethered to the woman's hand, he had the impression that Kelli would have taken off to go exploring.

Her eyes were as blue as her mother's. "Is this your house?" the girl asked.

He felt the corners of his mouth curving. There was something infectious about Kelli's inquisitive manner. "Yes."

She raised her eyes up the stairs to the second floor. "It looks big."

Philippe wondered if all this was spontaneous, or if the woman had coached her daughter to ask certain questions for her. Children's innocent inquiries were hard to ignore.

Deciding to assume that Kelli was her mother's shill, he addressed his answer to the woman instead of the child.

"It's not, really," he assured the blonde. "It looks a great deal bigger on the outside, but mine is just the middle house." He spread his hands wide to encompass the area. "This is actually three houses made to look like one."

The information created a tiny furrow on the woman's forehead, right between her eyes. She looked as if his words had annoyed her. "I'm familiar with the type," the woman replied softly.

"Good."

The lone word hung in midair between them like a damp curtain.

He'd never had a housekeeper before. As a matter of fact, he'd never interviewed anyone for any sort of position before and hadn't the slightest idea how to go about it now without sounding like a complete novice. Or worse, a complete idiot. The image didn't please him.

Clearing his throat again, Philippe pushed on. "Then you know there won't be much work involved."

The woman smiled as if she was sharing some secret joke with herself. She had a nice smile. Otherwise, he might have taken offense.

"No disrespect, Mr. Zabelle," she said as she appeared to slowly take stock of his living room and what she could see beyond it, "but I'll be the judge of that." She turned to face him. "Once you tell me exactly what it is you have in mind."

He had no idea why that would cause him to almost swallow his tongue. Maybe it was the way she looked at him or, more likely, the way she'd uttered that phrase. She certainly didn't remind him of any housekeeper he'd ever come across while living at his mother's house.

"Have you done this before?" he asked. In his experience, housekeepers were usually older women, more likely than not somewhat maternal looking. This one was neither and if there was one thing he wanted, it was someone experienced. But he was a fair man and willing to be convinced.

She looked at him as if he'd just insulted her. "Yes," she replied with more than a little feeling. "I have references. I can show them to you once we finish talking about the basics here."

He nodded at the information, although when he'd find the time to check her references was beyond him. Maybe he could get Alain or Remy to do it for him. Both had more free time than he did.

She was obviously waiting for him to define the requirements. He gave it his best shot. "Well, I won't be asking you to do anything you haven't done before."

That didn't come out quite right, he realized the minute he'd said it.

The blonde reinforced his impression. Blinking, she asked, "Excuse me?"

He must have said something wrong but hadn't the slightest idea what. There was no clue forthcoming from the woman's daughter either. Kelli seemed amused by the whole exchange. Maybe she wasn't a little girl after all, just a very short adult. Her face was certainly expressive enough to qualify.

Philippe tried again. "I mean, it'll be the usual. Some light dusting." He shrugged, thinking. "Shopping once a week."

The woman's mouth dropped open. And still managed to look damn sensual. It belatedly occurred to him that he still didn't even know her name. "I don't—"

"Do windows?" he completed her sentence. "That's okay, I have a service that comes by twice a year to wash my windows." There was no way he could reach the upper portion of some of them even if he did have the time, which he didn't. "I just need someone to clean up—nothing major," he assured her quickly, "because most of the time, I'm holed up in my office." He jerked a thumb toward the rear of the house. "And I'd rather you didn't come in there."

The woman shook her head, as if put off. "Mr. Zabelle, I think there's been some mistake."

He didn't want there to be some mistake. He wanted her to take the job. He couldn't see himself going through this process over and over again.

Philippe took a stab at the reason for her comment. "You're full-time, right?"

"When I work, yes."

Philippe paused, thinking. "I really don't need anyone fulltime."

"I think what you need is an interpreter." Her response confused him, but before he could tell her as much, she was saying, "When I start a job, Mr. Zabelle, I finish it."

Well, that was a good trait, he thought, but he still wasn't going to hire her full-time. "That's very admirable, but like I said, I'm only going to need someone once a week."

Rather than accept that, he saw her put her hands on her waist. "And why is that?"

Maybe this was a mistake after all. He could have gone to the store and back in the amount of time he'd spent verbally dancing around with this woman. "Because there won't be enough to keep you occupied," he told her tersely. "I'm pretty neat."

She shook her head as if to clear it. "What does your being neat have to do with it?"

"I realize you probably charge the same whether you're working for a slob or someone who's relatively neat—"

She cut him off before he could finish. "I charge according to what the client requests, Mr. Zabelle, not based on whether they're sloppy or neat."

That sounded a hell of a lot more personal than just cleaning his house.

Their eyes met and Philippe watched her for a long moment. The more he did, the less she looked like a housekeeper. Just what section had his ad landed in? And if it was what he was thinking, what was she doing bringing her daughter along on this so-called job interview?

His eyes narrowed slightly. "Did you get my number from the personals?"

He watched as her mouth formed as close to a

perfect *O* as he had ever seen. He saw her hand tightened around Kelli's.

"Mommy, you're squishing my fingers," the little girl protested.

"Sorry," she murmured, never taking her eyes off his face. She was looking at him as if she thought that perhaps she should be backing away. Quickly. "I got your number from my machine, Mr. Zabelle," she told him, her voice both angry and distant now.

Okay, he was officially lost. "Your machine?" That made no sense to him. "I called the newspaper this morning."

She cocked her head, as if that could help her make sense of all this somehow. "About?"

"The ad," he said, annoyed. Had she lost the thread of the conversation already? What kind of an attention span did she have?

"What ad?" she demanded. She sounded like someone on the verge of losing her temper.

Taking a breath, Philippe enunciated each word slowly, carefully, the way he would if he were talking to someone who was mentally challenged. "The… one…you're…here…about."

Her voice went up several levels. "I'm not here about any ad."

Suddenly, something unlocked in a distant part of his brain. Her voice was very familiar. He'd heard it before. Recently.

Philippe held up his hand, stopping her. "Hold it. Back up." He peered at her face intently, trying to jog his memory. Nothing. "Who are you, lady?"

A loud huff of air preceded the reply. When she spoke, it was through gritted teeth. "I'm J. D. Wyatt. You called me about remodeling your bathrooms."

And then it hit him. Like a ton of bricks. He knew where he'd heard that voice before—on the phone, last night. "*You're* J. D. Wyatt?"

J.D. drew herself up. He had the impression she'd been through this kind of thing before—and had no patience with it. "Yes."

He wanted to be perfectly clear in his understanding of the situation. "You're not here about the housekeeping job?"

"The housekeep—" Oh God, now it made sense. The weekly shopping, the cleaning. He'd made a natural mistake—and one that irked her. "No, I'm not here about the housekeeping job. I'm a contractor."

He thought back to what Vincent had said when he'd given him the card. "I thought I was calling a handyman."

J.D. shrugged. She'd lived in a man's world all of her life and spent most of her time struggling to gain acceptance. "A handy-person," she corrected.

The discomfort he'd been feeling grew. It was bad enough not being handy and feeling inferior to another man. Aesthetically speaking, all men might have been created equal, but not when it came to wielding a hacksaw. Feeling inferior to a woman with a tool belt? Well, that was a whole different matter. He wasn't sure he could handle it.

It felt like he'd been deceived. "What does the J.D. stand for?"

She eyed him for a long moment, as if debating whether or not to tell him. And then she did. "Janice Diane."

"So why didn't you just put that down on the card?" he asked. "You realize that's false advertising."

"My mama's not false!" Kelli piped up indignantly, moving between her mother and him.

"Kelli, hush," J.D. soothed. "It's okay." And then she looked at him and her sunny expression faded. "There's nothing false about it. Those are my initials."

"You know what I mean. By using them, you make people think that they're hiring a man."

That was the whole point, she thought. This man might look drop-dead gorgeous, but he was as dumb as a shoe—and probably had the soul to match. She spelled it out for him.

"People do not call someone named *Janice Diane* to fix their running toilets or renovate their flagstone fireplaces. They do, however, call someone named J.D. to do the same work. This world runs on preconceived notions, Mr. Zabelle. One of those notions is that men are handy, women are not. Your reaction just proved my point. You thought I was here to clean your house, not to renovate it."

She was right and he didn't like it, but he couldn't come up with a face-saving rebuttal. "Well, I—"

It wouldn't have mattered if he had, she wouldn't let him finish.

"I've been around tools all my life and I know what to do with them." She folded her arms before her. "Now, are you going to let your prejudice keep you from hiring the best handy-person you're ever going to come across in your life—at any price—or are you going to be a modern man and show me what exactly you need done around here?" It was a challenge, pure and simple. One she hoped he would rise to.

Out of the corner of her eye, Janice saw Kelli mimic her actions perfectly, folding her small arms before her.

Mother and daughter stood united, waiting for a reply.

Chapter Three

For what felt like an endless moment, two different reactions warred within Philippe, each striving for the upper hand.

Ever since he could remember, he'd had it drummed into his head—and had come to truly believe—that the only difference between men and women were that women had softer skin. Usually. His mother had enthusiastically maintained over and over again that women could do anything a man could except go to the bathroom standing up. And even there, she had declared smugly, women had the better method. At the very least, it was neater.

But there was another, equally strong reaction that beat within his chest. It was based on the deep-seated philosophy that men were the doers, the protectors in this dance of life. This notion had evolved very early in his life and had come from the fact that he'd been the responsible one in the family, the steadfast one. His mother flittered in and out of relationships, fell in and out of love, while he held down the fort, making sure that his brothers stayed out of trouble and went to school. And occasionally, when there was a need for it, his was the shoulder on which his mother would cry or vent.

He grew up believing that there were certain things that men did. They might be partners with women on a daily basis, but in times of crisis, the partnership tended to go from fifty-fifty to seventy-thirty, with the man taking up the slack.

And under that heading, but in a much looser sense, came the concept of being handy. Women weren't supposed to be handy, at least, not handier than the men of the species. Women were not the guardians of the tool belt, they were the nurturers.

Right now, as he vacillated between giving in to his pride and being fair, Philippe could almost hear his mother whispering in his ear.

"Damn it, Philippe, I raised you better than this. Give the girl a chance. She has a child, for heaven's sake. Besides, she's very easy on the eye. Not a bad little number to have around."

At the very least, it wouldn't hurt to have J.D. give him an estimate. If he didn't like it, that would be the end of that. Mentally, he crossed his fingers.

With a barely suppressed sigh, he nodded. "All right. Let me show you the bathroom."

Philippe began leading the way to the rear of the house, past the kitchen. Somehow, Kelli managed to wiggle in front of him just as they came to the bathroom that had begun it all, the one with the cracked sink.

Hands on either side of the doorjamb, Kelli peered into the room before her mother could stop her, then declared in a very adult, very disappointed voice, "Oh, it's not pretty." Turning around, she looked up at him with a smile that promised everything was going to be all right. "But don't worry, Mama can make it pretty for you. She's very good."

Philippe raised an eyebrow. "She your press agent?" he asked, amused despite himself as he nodded toward the little girl.

For the first time, he saw the woman in the well-fitting faded jeans smile. Janice ruffled her daughter's silky blond hair with pure affection. "More like my own personal cheering section."

An identical smile was mirrored on Kelli's lips. The resemblance was uncanny.

Stepping back to grab her mother's hand, Kelli proceeded to tug her into the small rectangular slightly musty room. "C'mon, Mommy, tell him what you're gonna do to make it look pretty."

Janice glanced over her shoulder toward the man she hoped was going to hire her and allow her to make this month's mortgage payment. "I don't think *pretty* is what Mr. Zabelle has in mind, honey."

Kelli pursed her lips together, clearly mulling over her mother's words. And then she raised her bright blue eyes up to look at his face, studying him intently as if she was trying to decide just what sort of creature he was.

"Everyone likes pretty," she finally declared with the firm conviction of the very young.

Philippe's experience with children was extremely limited. It really didn't go beyond his own rather adult childhood and the brothers he'd all but raised. All of that now residing in the distant past.

Too distant for him to really recall with any amount of clarity.

But since Kelli made decrees like a short adult, he treated her as such and said, "That all depends on what you mean by *pretty.*"

The smile on the rosebud mouth was back, spreading along it generously and banishing her momentary serious expression. This time, she looked up at her mother and giggled. "He's funny, Mommy."

Janice slipped her hand around Kelli's shoulders, stooping down to do so. "He's the client, Kel, and we don't talk about him as if he's not in the room when he's standing right beside us."

"Good rule to remember," Philippe approved, then decided to ask a question of his own. "You always bring your daughter along on interviews?"

Interviews. Janice had gotten to dislike the word. It made her feel as if she was being scrutinized. As if someone was passing judgment on her. There had been more than enough of that when she'd been growing up. Her father was always judging her—and finding her lacking. Besides, she took exception to Zabelle's question. It wasn't any of his business if Kelli came along or not as long as everything else was conducted professionally.

Without meaning to, she squared her shoulders. "My sitter had a date."

Philippe supposed that was a reasonable excuse, although the woman could have rescheduled. "Good for her."

"Him," she corrected. "Good for him," she added when he looked at her quizzically. "My sitter's my brother, Gordon."

Mentally, Philippe came to an abrupt halt. He was getting far more information than he either needed or wanted. If he did wind up hiring this woman to tinker and fix the couple of things that needed fixing, he wanted to keep their exchanges strictly to a business level.

But that wasn't going to be easy, he realized in the

next moment when the little girl took his hand in hers and brightly informed him, "I don't have a brother. Do you have one?"

He expected Kelli's mother to step in and admonish the little girl for talking so freely to a stranger. But there was nothing forthcoming from J.D. and Kelli was apparently waiting for him to give her an answer.

"Yes," he finally said. "Two."

"Do they live here, too?" Kelli asked. She seemed ready to go off in search of them.

He shifted his eyes toward the so-called handyperson. "Don't you think you should teach her not to be so friendly with strangers?"

Janice had never liked being told what to do. She struggled now to keep her annoyance out of her voice. The man probably meant well and he was, after all, a potential client.

But who the hell did he think he was, telling her how to raise her daughter?

She took a breath before answering, trying her best to sound calm. She was dealing with residual anxiety, as always when Gordon went out on a date. He had a very bad tendency to overdo things and shower his companions with gifts he couldn't afford.

When she finally spoke, it was in a low voice, the same voice he'd heard on the answering machine. "I don't see the need to make her paranoid if I'm around to watch her. Kelli knows enough not to talk to someone she doesn't know if she's alone—which she never is," Janice added firmly. "Besides," she continued, "Kelli's a very good judge of character."

Now that he found hard to believe. "And she's how old?"

He was mocking her, Janice thought. Probably thought she was one of those doting mothers who thought their kid walked on water. But Kelli seemed to have a radar when it came to nice people. She turned very shy around the other type.

"Age doesn't always matter," she told Zabelle. Gordon, for instance, had the impaired judgment of a two-month-old Labrador puppy. Everyone was his friend—until proven otherwise. The later happened far too often. He had a *V* on his forehead for victim and self-serving women could hone in on it from a fifty-mile radius. "Sometimes all it takes are good instincts." Something Gordon didn't seem to possess when it came to women. He fell prey to one gold digger after another. The sad part was that he never caught on. And if she said anything, her brother felt she was being a shrew.

It was hard to believe that he was the older one.

Because he'd asked and her mother hadn't answered, Kelli held up four fingers and bent her thumb to illustrate what she was about to say. "I'm four and three-quarters." She dropped her hand and then added in a stage whisper that would have made a Shakespearean actor proud, "Mama says I'm going on forty."

The unassuming remark made him laugh. "I can believe that."

"Why don't we get down to business?" Janice suggested. She wanted to wrap this up as quickly as possible, especially if it didn't lead anywhere. She hadn't had a chance to prepare dinner yet. That had been Gordon's job, but then Sheila, the latest keeper of his heart, had called and he'd forgotten everything else. When she'd come home from wrapping up a job, he'd all but run over her in his haste to leave the house.

"Good, you're finally home. Gotta run." And he did. Literally.

"Dinner?" she'd called after him.

"Yeah," he'd tossed over her shoulder. "I'm taking her out. Seems she's free after all."

Which had meant that whoever Sheila had planned to go out with had cancelled.

There'd been no time for Janice to prepare dinner before her appointment, so she'd tossed an apple to Kelli, strapped her into her car seat and driven over to the address she'd copied down. But now her stomach was making her pay for it by rumbling. She wished she'd grabbed an apple for herself.

"Fine with me," Philippe told her. He gestured toward the sink. Running the length of the sink from one end to the other, the crack was hard to miss. "I need that replaced."

Instead of looking at the sink, Janice slowly examined the bathroom, taking in details and cataloguing them in her head. Judging by appearances, no one had done anything to the oversized powder room with the undersized shower in about thirty years.

The dead giveaway was the carpet on the floor. It was very 1970s.

Finished assessing, she turned to him. "Looks to me as if you could stand to have the whole bathroom replaced."

He hadn't given any serious thought to any large-scale renovations, but he knew he wouldn't want them handled by a wisp of a woman. "Oh?"

She nodded as if he'd just agreed with her. "The tile is very bland," she pointed to the wall. "It dates the room, as does the carpet. And you're missing grout in several places." She indicated just where. "My guess is that it was probably scrubbed out over the years." She based her assumption on the fact that there didn't appear to be any visible mold. Left to their own devices, most men had bathrooms that doubled as giant petri dishes, growing several different strains of mold and fungus. "Whoever's been cleaning your bathroom has been doing an excellent job, but scrubbing does take its toll on tile and grout after a while."

He wasn't sure if she was giving him a compliment or trying to get him to volunteer more information about his personal life. In either case, he shrugged. "I just find things to spray on it—whenever I remember," he added, thinking of the last time he'd had the opportunity to go to the grocery store.

The tiny snippet of information impressed her. "A man who cleans his own bathroom." She said it the way someone might announce they'd just discovered a unicorn. "I'll have to have my brother come meet you."

That was the last thing he wanted—unless her brother was part of her crew. The second he had the thought, he realized she had somehow subtly gotten him to consider the idea of renovations rather than a simple replacement.

Still, maybe that wouldn't be such a bad thing. He looked at her in silence for a minute, then decided to ask a hypothetical question. "Okay, pure speculation."

"Yes?" she returned gamely, mentally crossing her fingers.

"If I were to do this bathroom over." And now that he thought of it, it did look pretty washed out and lifeless. "What would something like that run?"

There was no easy answer. She was surprised that he expected one—was he the type that liked having everything neatly pigeonholed? "That depends on what you'd want done."

Nothing until five minutes ago, he thought. "Nothing fancy," he said aloud. "Just replacing what's here with newer fixtures."

She glanced down at the worn short-shag carpeting that went from one wall to another. Why would anyone have ever considered that acceptable? "And tile for the floor."

That surprised him. J.D. had hit on the one thing

he'd been toying with having done—when he got around to it. He'd never cared for having a carpet in the bathroom. It got way too soggy from wet feet.

"And tile for the floor," he echoed, agreeing.

Well, at least they were beginning on the same page. "Different quality fixtures affect the total sum," she maintained.

"Ballpark figure," he requested, then amended it by saying, "what you'd charge for your labor, since I'm guessing the materials would cost me the same as you if I went and got them myself."

"More," she corrected. He looked at her quizzically. "Unless you just happen to have a contractor's license in your pocket."

He patted either pocket, causing Kelli to giggle. He realized he liked the sound of that. "Fresh out." He hooked his thumbs in the corners of his front pockets. "So I get a break hiring you?"

She didn't want to come across as pushy. People who applied too much pressure wound up losing their potential customers. It was the one thing she'd learned by watching her father. "Or any contractor."

He couldn't ask what the materials would come to until he decided on the materials. But he could ask her about her fee. He'd never liked flying blind. "Okay, what's your bottom line?"

This time the giggle needed two hands to keep it restrained—and still it came through. "Mama doesn't have a line on her bottom," Kelli piped up, her eyes dancing with amusement.

For a second, as he stared down into the eyes of the improbable woman behind the initials, he'd almost lost his train of thought. He'd definitely forgotten that her daughter was there.

Philippe laughed now at the serious expression that had slipped over what had been an incredibly sunny little face. "I didn't mean—"

"The bottom line means what things will cost," Janice explained to her daughter, speaking as if Kelli were a business associate being trained on the job.

Maybe she was, he thought, then dismissed the idea as ridiculous. It was way too soon to be training that little girl to do anything but enjoy life to the fullest and he had a sneaking suspicion those lessons had already been given.

"Oh," was all he trusted himself to say.

Janice turned toward him and after pausing a moment to take things in again and, doing a few mental calculations in her head, she gave him a quote.

He stared at her incredulously. "You're serious," he asked.

"Yes, why?"

The why was because she'd given him a bid that sounded much too low, even if it did only include her labor and not the cost of materials. "How do you stay in business with fees like that?"

She breathed a silent sigh of relief. He wasn't one of those tightwads who thought everything had to be haggled down.

"Low overhead," Janice quipped without hesitation. She ventured a little further. Once people got their feet wet, they usually decided they wanted something else done. She began with the logical choice. "Is this the only bathroom you want renovated?"

"I didn't even want this one renovated," he informed her, then abruptly stopped. The quote she'd given him was more than reasonable, coming in far lower than he would have expected. He wasn't up on the price of bathroom renovations, per se, but one of the people who marketed his software packages had just had a bathroom redone. The man had proudly given him a quote that had taken his breath away. Philippe remembered thinking that his maternal grandfather had paid less for his house when he'd bought it forty years ago than the man had paid to have his bathroom upgraded. "The other two are upstairs."

"You have three bathrooms?" Kelli asked gleefully, her eyes huge.

He had no idea why the little girl would find that a source of wonder. "Yes."

"We only have two," she confided, then leaned into him and added, "And Uncle Gordon is always in one."

Janice saw Zabelle raise his eyes and look at her quizzically. She didn't want him thinking that Gordon was strange. "My brother is staying with us while he gets back on his feet."

Kelli's silken blond curls fairly bounced as she turned her head around to face her. "Uncle Gordon gets on his feet every day, Mama."

It was an expression, but she didn't feel like trying to explain that to Kelli right now. Instead, she stroked Kelli's hair and said, "Only for short periods of time, baby."

Instinctively, Janice glanced at the man whose house they were in. She recognized curiosity when she saw it, even though she had her doubts that the man even knew the expression had registered on his face. She felt obligated to defend her brother against what she guessed this man had to be thinking.

"My brother's had a tough time of it lately." *Lately* encompassed the period from his birth up to the present day, she added silently.

Zabelle seemed to take the information in stride. "At least he has family."

The comment took her by surprise. Janice hadn't expected the man to say that. It was by all accounts a sensitive observation.

Maybe the man wasn't half bad after all.

"Yes," she agreed with a note of enthusiasm in her voice as she came to the landing, "he does. By the way," she said, leaning outside the bathroom wall and looking at him, "I noticed your kitchen."

This time, he thought, he was ready for her. Ready

to put a firm lid on this before it escalated into something that necessitated his moving out of the house for several weeks. "And?"

"Could stand to have a bit of a face-lift as well."

"This was about a cracked sink," Philippe reminded her.

It was never just about a cracked sink. By the time that stage was reached, other things were in need of fixing and replacing as well. "I thought that the oldest son of Lily Moreau would be more open to productive suggestions—even if they do come from a woman who owns a tool belt." She saw the surprise in his eyes grow. "I have access to the Internet," she pointed out glibly. "And I try to learn as much as I can about potential clients before I meet with them."

He noticed that she said the word *potential* as if it was to be discarded while the word *client* had a healthy amount of enthusiasm associated with it. The woman was obviously very sure of herself.

Even so, he didn't like having his mind made up for him.

Chapter Four

"So, are you going to do his bathrooms, Mama?" Kelli piped up as they finally drove away from Philippe Zabelle's house.

Easing her foot on the brake as she approached a red light, Janice glanced up into the rearview mirror. Kelli sat directly behind her in her car seat, something she suffered with grace. Car seats were required for the four and under set, something she insisted she no longer was inasmuch as she was four and three-quarters.

Kelli was waving her feet at just a barely lesser tempo than a hummingbird flapped its wings. Any second now, her daughter would lift off, seat and all.

Energy really was wasted on the young. "Yes. I'll be redoing them."

"And the kitchen, too?" There was excitement in Kelli's voice.

It never failed to amaze her just how closely Kelli paid attention. Another child wouldn't have even noticed what was going on. Too bad Kelli couldn't give Gordon lessons.

"Yes, the kitchen, too."

That had been touch and go for a bit, but then she'd managed to convince Zabelle there were wonderful possibilities available to him. She wasn't trying to line her pockets so much as she felt a loyalty to give her client the benefit of her expertise and creative eye.

In actuality, the whole house could do with a makeover, but she was content to have gotten this far. Three bathrooms and a kitchen. Now all she needed was to get to her computer and start sketching.

"And what else?" Kelli wanted to know.

God, but the little girl sounded so grown up at times, Janice thought. Her foot on the accelerator, she drove through the intersection and made a right at the next corner. "That's it for now, honey."

Despite the fact that she was a good craftsperson and she had a contractor's license, obtained in the days when there'd been an actual decent-sized company to work for—her father's—Janice knew she worked at a definite disadvantage. Philippe Zabelle was not the only man skeptical about hiring a woman to handle his renovations. Her own father had been like that, even though she'd proven herself to him over and over again.

He always favored Gordon over her.

She supposed she was partially to blame for that. Because she loved him, she always covered up for Gordon when he messed up, doing his work for him so that he wouldn't have to endure their father's wrath.

Even now, the memory of that wrath made her involuntarily shiver.

Sisterly love ultimately caused her to be shut out. When he died, her father had left the company to Gordon. There wasn't even a single provision about her—or her baby—in Jake Wyatt's will.

It was a cold thing to do, she thought now, her hands tightening on the steering wheel as she eked through the next light.

Gordon had had as much interest in the company as a muskrat had in buying a winter coat from a major department store. Without their father around to cast his formidable shadow, Gordon became drunk on freedom. He turned his attention away from the business and toward the pursuit of his one true passion—women. A year and a half after their father died the company belonged to the bank because of the loans Gordon drew against Wyatt Construction, and she, a widow with a young child and three-quarters of a college degree, had to hustle in order to provide for herself and Kelli.

At first, she'd been desperate to take anything that came her way. She quickly discovered that she hated sales, hated being a waitress and the scores of other dead-end endeavors she undertook in order to pay the bills. Dying to get back to the one thing she knew she was good at and loved doing, she'd advertised in the local neighborhood paper, posted ads on any space she could find on community billboards and slowly, very slowly, got back into the game.

But every contracting job she eventually landed was preceded by a fair amount of hustling and verbal tap dancing to convince the client that she was every bit as good as the next contractor—and more than likely better because she'd been doing it for most of her life. She was the one, not Gordon, who liked to follow their father around, lugging a toolbox and mimicking his every move. Dolls held no interest for her, drill bits did.

"Mama," the exasperated little voice behind her rose another octave as Kelli tried to get her attention, "I asked you a question."

Their eyes met in the mirror. Janice did her best to look contrite. "Sorry, baby, I was thinking about something else for a second. What do you want to know?"

"Is he gonna want more?"

For a second, Janice had lost the thread of the conversation Kelli was conducting. "Who?"

She heard Kelli sigh mightily. She pressed her lips together, trying not to laugh. Sometimes it almost felt as if their roles were reversed and Kelli was the mom while she was the kid.

"The man with the pretty painting, Mama."

Now Janice really did draw a blank. "Painting?" she echoed, trying to remember if she'd noticed a painting anywhere. She came up empty.

"Yes. In the living room." Kelli carefully enunciated every word, as if afraid she would lose her mother's attention at any second. "There was a big blue lake and trees and—didn't you see it, Mama?" Kelli asked impatiently.

"Apparently not."

Art was definitely Kelli's passion. The little girl had been drawing ever since she could hold a pencil in her hand. The swirls and stick figures that first emerged quickly gave way to recognizable shapes and characters at an amazingly young age. Beautiful characters that seemed to have personalities radiating from them. It was her fervent dream to send her daughter to a good art school and encourage the gift she had. Kelli was never going to go through what she had, wasn't going to have her ability dismissed, devalued and ignored.

"I'll have to go look at it the next time I'm there," she told her daughter, then paused before asking, "You are talking about Mr. Zabelle's house, right?"

Kelli sighed again. "Right." And then she got back to what she'd said initially. "Maybe he'll want you to do more when he sees how good you are."

Bless her, Janice thought. "That would be nice." To

that end, she'd left the man with a battery of catalogues, some of which dealt with rooms other than the kitchen and the bath. A girl could always hope.

"If you do more, will we have enough for a pony?" Kelli asked.

Ah, the pony issue again. Another passion, but one that had far less chance of being realized. At least for the present. But she played along because it was easier that way than squelching Kelli's hopes. "Not yet, honey. Ponies need a special place to stay and special food to eat, remember?"

The golden head bobbed up and down. "When will we have enough for a pony?"

"I'll let you know," Janice promised.

Making another turn, she looked down at her left hand. She still missed the rings that had been there. The ones she'd been forced to pawn in January to pay bills. January was always a slow month as far as business was concerned. The month that people focused on trying to pay off the debts they'd run up during the Christmas season. Room additions and renovation moved to the back of the line.

If there was any money leftover after the Zabelle job, she was going to put it toward getting her rings out of hock. The stone on the engagement ring wasn't very large, but Gary had picked it out for her and she loved it.

A bittersweet feeling wafted over her. She and Gary

had gotten engaged one week, then married two weeks later because he'd discovered that his unit was being sent clear across to the other side of the world to fight. He never returned under his own power.

She fought back against the feeling that threatened to overwhelm her. Five years and it was still there, waiting for an unguarded moment. Waiting to conquer her. Again.

But you did what you had to do in order to keep going. Pawning her rings had been her only option at the time. Bills needed to be paid. The rings didn't mean very much if there wasn't a roof over Kelli's head. After Gordon had lost the business, she was very mindful of not putting her daughter and herself in jeopardy of losing the things that were most important to them. That meant not waiting until the last minute before taking measures to safeguard home and hearth.

"Can we go out to eat, Mama?"

Trust Kelli to ground her, she thought. She felt guilty about letting herself get sidetracked. "You bet, kid. You get to pick the place."

That required absolutely no thought on Kelli's part. "I wanna go to the pizza place."

Pizza was by far her daughter's favorite food. Janice laughed. "You are going to turn into a pizza someday, Kel."

Her comment was met with a giggle. The sound warmed Janice's heart.

* * *

"Where's your cheering section?" Philippe asked two evenings later when he found only J.D. on his doorstep. He leaned over the threshold and looked around in case the little girl was hiding.

"Home," she informed him. He stepped back to let her in. "My babysitter doesn't have a date tonight." When Gordon's newest flame found out about his cash-flow problems—basically that it wasn't even trickling, much less flowing—she quickly became history. When she'd left to come here, Kelli and Gordon were watching the Disney Channel together. "Kelli wanted to come along." But this was going to involve long discussions of fees and she preferred not subjecting her daughter to that. "I think she likes you."

Walking into the living room, Janice abruptly stopped before the framed twenty-four by thirty-six painting hanging on the wall.

My God, it was so large, how had she missed that the first time?

Because she was focusing on landing this job, she thought. She tended to have tunnel vision when it came to work, letting nothing else distract her. Although she had to admit that she had noticed Philippe Zabelle would never be cast as the frog in the Grimm Brothers' "The Frog Prince."

Janice redirected her attention to the painting. It was

breath-taking. Kelli had an eye, all right. "I know she likes your painting."

"My *mother's* painting," he corrected, in case she thought that he had painted it. "I'll let my mother know she has a new fan. I know she'll be delighted to hear that she's finally cracked the under-ten set. Most kids don't even notice painting unless they're forcibly dragged to an art museum."

Forcibly dragged. Zabelle sounded as if he was speaking from experience. Had his mother forced art on him, attempted to make him appreciate it before he was ready? She'd taken Kelli to the Museum of Contemporary Art in Los Angeles when the little girl had still been in a stroller. Kelli had been enthralled.

"Most kids didn't start drawing when they are barely three," she countered.

He led the way to the kitchen table. She had paperwork for him, he surmised. He eyed her quizzically. "Drawing?"

Pride wiggled through her like a deep-seated flirtation. "Drawing."

He assumed she was being loose with her terminology. He remembered his brothers trying to emulate their mother. Best efforts resembled the spiral trail left by the Tasmanian devil.

"You mean as in scribbling?"

"No," she said firmly, "I mean as in drawing."

He laughed softly, pulling out a chair for her. "Spoken like a true doting mother."

Janice took mild offense. Not for herself, but for Kelli. Her daughter deserved better than that. "I'll show you."

"You carry around her portfolio?" he asked incredulously. When he saw her reaching into the battered briefcase that contained the contracts she'd brought with her for him to sign, Philippe realized that only one of them thought that what he'd just said was a joke. She snapped open the locks and lifted the lid. "You're kidding."

Janice didn't bother answering him. A picture, as they said, is worth a thousand words. She could protest that Kelli was as talented as they come, but he needed to see for himself. So, lifting up several manila folders and her trusty laptop, she took Kelli's latest drawing out of the case. It was of a white stallion from Kelli's favorite cartoon show.

Very carefully, she placed the drawing on top of her briefcase and then turned it toward him.

Philippe's eyes widened. "You're not kidding," he murmured.

As he admired the drawing, he shook his head. There was no way the bouncy little thing he'd met two nights ago had done this. He sincerely doubted that she could sit still long enough to finish it.

He made contact with J.D. "You did that."

She laughed softly. "I wish. My ability doesn't go beyond drawing rectangles and squares. I can do blueprints," she concluded. "I can't do horses."

Zabelle took the drawing from her. She curled her fingers into her hand to keep from grabbing it back. She was very protective of Kelli and that protectiveness extended to her daughter's things and her talent. It was a trait she would have to rein in if Kelli was ever going to grow up to be an independent adult.

Philippe gave her one last chance to withdraw her statement. "She really drew this."

"She really drew that," Janice told him proudly.

For the first half of his life, when his mother wasn't immersed in the creation of her own work or either nurturing along a new relationship or burying an old one, she had tried her very best to get him to follow in her footsteps. While he shared her talent to a degree, he had rebelled and steadfastly refused.

His reasons were simple. Art was her domain, he wasn't going to venture into it. Nor was he ready to stand in her shadow, struggling to be his own person. He needed a medium, a venue that belonged to him alone. A path apart from hers.

But that didn't keep him from admiring someone else's gift. "Can I hang onto this for a little while?" he asked abruptly.

The request caught Janice by surprise. "Why?"

The man just didn't strike her as the post-it-on-the-refrigerator type, which was where this had been until, on a whim, she'd packed it in with her contracts. She'd told herself that it would act as a good luck talisman.

"I'd like to show this to my mother the next time she flies in here."

"Your mother's out of state?" she asked, a little confused.

"No." He pulled out a chair and straddled it, resting his arms on the back. "She's right here in Bedford, California. My mother's a little larger than life and she gives the impression of flying whenever she enters a room."

"Oh, I see." She found herself wanting to meet this dynamo. Her own mother had left a long time ago, before she ever really established a relationship with her. She just remembered a tall, thin woman with light blond hair and an air of impatience about her. Eventually that impatience had led her out the door, a note on the kitchen table left in her wake. "Well, then I guess it's all right. If she asks me about it, I'll just tell Kelli that the lady who painted the landscape in your living room is going to look at her drawing."

"Why not just tell her that I have it? Why give her this longer version?"

She could see he hadn't dealt much with children. "Would you like a short person laying siege to your house?" she deadpanned. "The minute I tell her that you have it, that you thought it was good, there will be no peace," she amended, her eyes on his. "Kelli will want to know what your mother thought of it, if she liked it. She'll want to know what your mother thought was good about it. And that's only after she quizzes me about your reaction to her work. Trust me, my way is better."

She sounded as if she was speaking about an adult, a thoughtful adult. The woman was giving her daughter way too much credit. And yet…

Philippe looked down at the drawing again. He had to admit he was in awe. "I don't know all that much about kids, but your daughter seems like one very unusual little girl."

Janice laughed. Now there was an understatement. "That she is."

Reaching for her briefcase again, this time to take the contracts out, she accidentally knocked the case off the table. Half the papers flew out. They both bent down at the same time to retrieve what had fallen; they both reached for the case and folders at the exact same moment. Which was how their fingers managed to brush against each other's.

It was, at best, a scene from a grade-B romantic movie, circa 1950. There was absolutely no reason to feel a jolt, electrifying or otherwise. And yet, there it was. Jolting. Electrifying. Fleeting, granted, but still very much there. Completely unexpected and zipping its way along the skin of her arms and simultaneously swirling up along the back of her neck.

Janice caught her breath, trying to make her pulse slow down. The last time she'd been with a man was three years ago. That even had been a terrible mistake, but it seemed like the right thing to do at the time.

But this, this was deeply seated in deprivation, not anything else. Deprivation, because she'd been leading the kind of life that would have made a crusty nun proud. But this small, accidental encounter had definitely rattled her cage.

She did her best to appear unaffected, as if, for a moment, her insides hadn't just turned to jelly.

"Thanks." Straightening, she picked up the contracts—one for each room—and placed them on the table. "Let's go over these, shall we?" she asked, her throat feeling uncomfortably tight. "I want to make sure I've got everything right. I don't want you finding that you're in for any surprises."

Too late, he thought. Because his reaction to her had already more than surprised him. But he put a lid on his thoughts and smiled at her. "Don't you like surprises?"

"I do, but my clients don't—not when it comes to cost, at any rate."

He rose, crossing to the refrigerator. "Would you like something to drink?" he asked.

The room—the house from what she could see—looked exactly the same as it did the other day. The man really was rather neat. Or had he found that housekeeper he'd mistaken her for?

"Diet soda—if you have any."

"As a matter of fact, I do." He'd gone to the store

earlier today and picked up a six pack. He had no idea what possessed him to do that because neither he nor his brothers nor any of his friends drank diet soda.

Maybe he'd just anticipated J.D., he decided, returning to the table with a can of diet soda. He placed a glass next to it.

Janice popped open the can and, ignoring the glass, took a long sip before speaking. "The hunt for a housekeeper, did you find one?" She set the can back down, wrapping her hands around it.

Philippe shrugged, straddling the chair again and pulling it closer to the table. "I decided to pull the ad."

"Oh?" she tried to sound casual. "Why?"

"Well, if the house is going to look like the site of the next demolition derby, that kind of negates the need for a housekeeper right now." A beer, he needed a beer. If he was going to go on staring into eyes the color of sky, he was going to need something to fortify him. Philippe made his way back to the refrigerator. "I'll hire one once things are back to normal."

Whatever that is, he added silently.

Chapter Five

He hadn't called.

Janice sighed, staring at the calendar on the kitchen wall depicting various breeds of puppies. Philippe Zabelle hadn't called—not on her land line, not on her cell. There were no messages waiting for her. She'd checked. Frequently.

Damn.

It'd been a little more than a week since the man had signed the contracts to have work done on his house. At the time, she'd noted he took the quotes in stride, not quibbling over any of the charges for demolition, cleanup and construction.

Maybe the reason Zabelle hadn't bothered quibbling was because he'd had no intentions of seeing the project move any further beyond his signing the contracts for each of his bathrooms and kitchen.

Eight days.

She'd finished the room extension she'd been doing for the Gilhooleys in Tustin. Faced with spare time, she'd gone to St. Cecelia's and done some handiwork there, replacing a window at the school, refitting a door at the priest's residence and fixing the hole in the roof where four tiles had blown away in the last storm. She'd finished that two days ago.

Right now, she was between jobs and at very loose ends. Janice had never done leisure well, never learned how to sit still for long, especially not when there were bills to pay.

And Gordon wasn't helping any, she thought, glancing over toward him accusingly. Her big brother was part of the problem, definitely not part of the solution. At the moment, he was lying on her sofa, dozing in front of the TV set. There was a baseball game droning on in the background. The Dodgers were losing.

Welcome to the club.

She sighed. The only one being productive around here at the moment was Kelli, who had spread out her paint set on the dining room table and was painting a woodland scene.

She needed to get that girl an easel, Janice thought. As soon as there was money for things like that.

Frustrated, she walked over to the sofa and shook Gordon's shoulder. It had no effect. Her brother went right on sleeping. Subtlety was obviously not working, so she doubled up her fist and punched him in the arm.

Gordon jolted awake.

"Hey!" he cried in protest, grabbing his arm where she'd made contact.

Gordon had never been one to endure pain stoically. "I hardly tapped you."

"You have a punch like a welterweight champion," he complained, looking at his arm as if he expected it to fall off. "What's wrong with you?"

"Everything. Look, Gordon." She sank down on the arm on the far end of the sofa. "I know you're going through a rough patch right now," she acknowledged charitably, "but you're going to have to help out here a little."

"I do," he protested indignantly. When she looked at him, mystified, he nodded over toward Kelli. "I watch the pip-squeak."

Janice pressed her lips together, struggling not to point out that their financial difficulties were largely because of him. "I meant help out with the expenses."

His eyebrows drew together over the bridge of his nose. "How?"

Wow, was it really that hard for him to connect the dots? "Get a job, Gordon. Get a job."

He sighed, as if that was a goal he aspired to, but wasn't quite able to reach just yet. "I'm still trying to find myself, J.D."

"Good news," she declared. "I found you. You're on the sofa. Now get off it and get yourself a damn job, Gordon."

"And do what?" he challenged.

She threw up her hands. "Sell ties at a major department store, wait on tables at Indigo's, become a bank teller. Anything." When Gordon made no response, she added through gritted teeth, "The way I did when you torpedoed Wyatt Construction right out from under me."

The look he gave her said she'd severely wounded him by bringing the past up. "I don't want to take just anything, J.D."

Easy for him to say. He had *never* hustled for a job. On those occasions when she landed a remodeling assignment that required more than just one person, she hired him on to help and, for the most part, things worked out. But the rest of the time, he seemed content to be "looking for himself" and doing absolutely nothing. Well, it couldn't continue.

Getting up, she crossed to him and lowered her face so that it was level to his. "You like to eat, don't you? Have a roof over your head? Shower daily? News flash, big brother. The best things in life *aren't* free."

He ignored the fact that she was now in his face. "When did you get so mercenary?"

"When you abdicated the position of adult and

became my other child," she retorted. If anything, she thought of him as being younger than Kelli.

"Ouch." Gordon cringed dramatically, as if ducking a blow. "Just because you're not working, don't take it out on me."

"I'm not taking it out on you," she countered, her patience dangerously low. "I just want you to pull your load. I just—" Exasperated, she waved her hand at him. "Oh, never mind."

"Okay then—" he settled back against the pillow, stretching his legs out before him "—maybe if I try hard, I can get back to the dream you so rudely terminated for me."

The temptation to smother him with his pillow was tremendous. She struggled to calm herself down. Janice knew her brother didn't mean anything by this and he really was having a rough time of it. Gordon seemed to fail at everything he tried, but she was bound and determined to keep him from sliding into some sort of black hole and dwelling there for the remainder of his life. He needed to stand up on his own two feet—the very minute he took them out of a certain part of his posterior.

And she supposed he was right in his own strange way. She *was* taking out her frustration over her forced inactivity on him. She had a perfectly good job lined up with some very nice additions, but she was stuck in first gear until Zabelle called her.

Or she found out what the holdup was.

The best way to do that was to beard the lion in his den. And she knew where the lion lived.

Janice abruptly made her way over to her daughter. "Sweetie," she called out. After taking another stroke the little girl stopped and glanced up at her. "I've got to go out for a while. Keep an eye on your Uncle Gordon for me, okay?"

Her request was met with a sunny smile. "You can count on me, Mama."

"I know." She kissed the top of Kelli's head. "More than on him," Janice added under her breath as she left the room.

She briefly thought about changing, but then decided that there was no point. This was the way she looked when she was working and, besides, she wasn't trying to impress Zabelle with her looks, just with her talent and her ability to get the job done in record time. Which she couldn't do if she didn't get started, she thought angrily.

This was why contractors took on more than one job at a time, she decided, getting behind the wheel of her 4x4. So that they wouldn't have to waste precious days with any downtime, some contractors would sign on for two, three jobs concurrently. But that had never been the way she operated. She believed in giving each job her complete, undivided attention from start to finish, finishing it and *then* moving on, not playing musical houses and going from one job to another as if they were all part of some kind of life-size round-robin.

She'd developed all the skills needed for this kind of work—all except for the tough hide. Ignoring the needs and requirements of others to satisfy her own just wasn't her style.

Janice knew, for instance, that she should be harder on Gordon, that maybe what he needed was a swift kick in the seat to get him moving and to make him repentant for losing the company, but she couldn't get herself to do it. Besides, she didn't see how making him feel guilty about losing the company would help since it would all be after the fact and it wouldn't accomplish anything. It certainly wouldn't get the company back.

It had taken her a while to come to grips with the loss. But, as always, she'd rallied and told herself that the company was not something that the bank held a deed to, the company was her—and Gordon when she could light a fire under him and get him to help.

At the time of her father's death, the company had included eight other men, men who had since gone on to work for other contractors, or left the area or even the business. But they were just the craftsmen. She was the heart of it, she was the blood that pumped through its veins.

And she wasn't going anywhere.

"You're not kidding," she murmured to herself as the irony of the phrase hit her. She turned her truck down Zabelle's street. She'd never get anywhere if jobs kept drying up on her.

Well, she wasn't about to let this one dry up, at least not without knowing the reason why. He owed her that much.

The house where Philippe Zabelle resided was located on a through street. It was part of a community of townhomes made to resemble well-spaced single dwellings that had lawns like lush green carpets. Bedford was considered to be one of the more upscale cities within Southern California. None of the neighborhoods were allowed to run down. Everything looked new or at least lovingly cared for. There was an abundance of pride within the city that kept its homes neat and looking their best.

Parking her car by the curb, Janice marched up the dozen or so white cement stairs that led up to the front door and knocked. First once, then twice and then a third time.

Nothing.

Maybe she should have called first, she thought. But if she had called and Zabelle had told her not to come, she would have lost the advantage of talking to him face to face. She always did better in person than over the phone.

Janice raised her hand to knock one more time.

"Looking for Philippe?"

Startled, her hand still raised, she swung around and found a tall, good-looking, dark-haired man with an easy smile and kind eyes standing to her left. She hadn't even heard him approach. Belatedly, she dropped her hand, realizing that, had he been standing any closer to her, she would have wound up punching him.

"Yes," she said when she regained possession of her voice. "I guess he's not home."

"Oh, he's in there," the man assured her. "He just tends to slip into another world when he's working. Doesn't see or hear anything else but what's on the screen in front of him."

"Dedicated," she commented.

The man smiled, amused. "One way of looking at it." Taking out a key, he unlocked the front door, pushed it open, then stood back. "Go ahead," he urged, gesturing toward the inside of the house.

She hung back. "I don't know if I should just walk in."

"I do it all the time." A grin flashed as he pocketed the key and he extended his hand to her. "Hi, I'm Georges. Philippe's brother," he added.

"Oh." Realizing that she was standing there like a bump on a log, Janice slipped her hand into his and shook it.

Georges's dark blue eyes were bright with curiosity as they swept over her. There was something unobtrusive about the way he did it. She took no offense. "And you are?"

"J. D. Wyatt," she told him, then added, "I'm supposed to do some work on your brother's house."

Recognition entered his eyes. "Oh, right, you're the

one Vincent mentioned." And then, as his own words registered, he seemed to do a mental double take. "You're J.D.?"

She smiled, removing her hand from his. This was the reaction she was accustomed to. "Not exactly what you expected, right?"

Rather than look embarrassed, he grinned. The man was charming, she thought. His brother could probably stand to pick up a few pointers—not that that mattered in the scheme of things, she reminded herself.

"Only in my better dreams," he told her. "Philippe didn't mention that he actually hired anyone, only that he was thinking about it."

That didn't bode well, Janice thought. Had Zabelle changed his mind after all? He'd signed contracts, but there was always a way around that if a person was clever and she didn't have the money for a lawyer to fight him on this anyway. Served her right from not insisting on getting a check right up front, right after Zabelle had signed on the dotted lines.

"But then," Georges added quickly, "Philippe doesn't say that much of anything, especially when he's in the middle of a project."

She had a feeling that Zabelle's brother was just trying to make her feel better. She examined him more closely. As brothers, they were more different than alike, she decided. "What does he do, your brother?"

"A little bit of everything." There was no missing the

pride in the man's voice. "But officially, Philippe's a computer programmer. Right now, he's designing software packages for online advertisers."

She glanced toward the opened door. They still had not gone inside. "And he works at home?"

Georges nodded. "Turns into a regular hermit when he's in the middle of designing something." He walked in, then turned when she didn't follow him. "C'mon, let's track him down."

When she'd gotten behind the wheel, she had been completely fired up. But on the way over, some of that fire had dissipated. It was one thing to confront the man at his door and read him an abbreviated version of the riot act about wasting her time, it was another to go from room to room, looking for him and running the risk of possibly catching him in a way he wouldn't want to be caught. God knew she wouldn't have appreciated having someone skulking around her house, looking for her.

She forced a smile to her lips. "Why don't you find him for me?" she suggested. Because he was looking at her expectantly, she ventured a few steps into the house, then indicated the living room. "I'll be right here, waiting for you."

The smile on his lips washed over her, leaving no part untouched. She really, really had to start dating again. Either that or begin working out rigorously—which she'd be doing if she were working, she silently insisted, bringing the argument full circle.

"Have it your way," Georges said. Turning, he faced the rear of the house and called out, "Hey, Philippe, where're you hiding?"

Still standing, Janice knotted her fingers together, feeling incredibly awkward. She closed her eyes for a second, trying to frame her first words to Zabelle under the present circumstances.

Georges had no sooner left the area than Philippe walked in from the kitchen. He stopped abruptly when he saw that there was a woman standing in the living room. The math equations that he'd been mentally grappling with receded as recognition set in.

J.D.

That still didn't answer what she was doing here. Or how she'd gotten in. He was damn certain he'd locked the front door. "Did I miss seeing cat burglar on your résumé?"

Her eyes flew open. Surprise and embarrassment took equal possession of her features. The resulting color was rather intriguing.

"I knocked," Janice protested.

He was pretty sure he hadn't heard anyone knocking, but he gave her the benefit of the doubt. Because of where his office was located, he probably wouldn't have heard the approach of the Four Horsemen, either.

"And then broke in?" he guessed.

"No," she protested quickly. The color in her cheeks rose up another notch. "Your brother let me in."

Both of his brothers were a bit too free about coming

and going from his place, but then, he supposed he should count himself lucky. It could have been his mother and there would have been no end to her questions. To J.D.

"Which one?" he asked mildly.

"He said his name was Georges." Curiosity got the better of her. "You have more than one?"

The shrug was careless. He wasn't about to be sidetracked. "I like having a spare. What are you doing here?"

She heard the slight tone of irritation in his voice. Any apology she was about to tender vanished. He was on the offensive? He didn't have the right to take the offensive. If anything, he was supposed to be on the *de*fensive, explaining why he'd kept her dangling the way he had.

Janice forgot about being uncomfortable and invading the man's space, and thought about being made to play hide and seek with her ever-growing stack of bills.

"I'm here to find out why you're welching," she said without preamble.

He stared at her, dumbfounded. "Welching?"

Okay, maybe that was a tad too harsh. She rephrased. "We had a deal, remember?"

"Yes, of course I remember. Frankly, I was wondering why you hadn't gotten started." He'd been too bogged down with a glitch in the program to notice during the day, but at night it would hit him that she hadn't called or shown up. By the time it registered, it was always too late for him to call and investigate.

She stared at him incredulously. He was serious. Either that or playing her for a fool. For the moment, she ignored the latter and began to talk to him as if he were mentally challenged. "I can't get started until you tell me what you picked out."

His response told her that she'd guessed correctly. The man had no clue. "Picked out?"

"The tile," she prompted. "Picked out the tile." She didn't see a light dawning in his eyes. How could he be that obtuse?

Again, Philippe shrugged. The mundane had little hold on him. "I don't know. I thought you were supposed to handle all that. I was okay with the drawings," he reminded her.

That was for the redesign of the kitchen and the bathrooms. That didn't take any of the materials into account.

"Yes, you were," she enunciated each word slowly, "but I don't know what color you want. What kind of cabinets you'd like to put in or even what kind of tile you want me to use."

He looked at her for a long moment, as if the words were slipping into his brain one at a time and he was processing them. "Tile comes in kinds?"

Having dealt with this world all of her life, it was impossible for Janice to imagine that anyone was ignorant of this sort of thing. Especially anyone who appeared to be intelligent. "Have you even been to a tile store?"

"No."

"Okay, baby steps," she murmured, more to herself. She made a spur of the moment decision. "All right, I'll take you." She just needed to call home and make sure that Gordon wasn't about to run off somewhere and forget that he had a niece to watch over.

Zabelle still didn't seem to be following her. "Take me where?"

"To a tile store."

Or two or three, she added silently, keeping that to herself. She guessed that if the man were told that this was a process that took most people several afternoons, he would balk and make excuses why he couldn't go.

His eyes narrowed. It didn't look encouraging. "When?"

"Now." It was half a query, half a direct order.

He shook his head. "I can't go now. I'm in the middle of something."

"How long before you're not in the middle of something?" she asked.

Philippe thought for a second. The deadline had been moved just yesterday. He'd never been comfortable about rushing through a project. That was his name on the cover and his reputation meant a great deal to him. "End of November."

Janice looked at him, stunned. November was three months away. She couldn't stretch things out until then. "Look, if you're trying to break the contracts—"

"Go with the lady," Georges said, picking that moment to walk in. "A few hours away from the drawing board might recharge your batteries."

Philippe began to protest that Georges didn't know what he was talking about. Georges was a doctor, not a designer. He had no idea what was involved in the process. But then he shrugged. The sooner he agreed and got this over with, the sooner the woman would be busy working and out of his hair.

He looked at J.D. "How fast can you get me there?" he wanted to know.

He'd done a one-eighty so fast, she felt as if she'd just sustained a severe case of whiplash. "Fast," she volunteered. Then, because she sensed he'd appreciate it, added, "But I'll try not to break any speed limits." As she spoke, she reached for her car keys and headed toward the front door. Turning, she nodded at Georges, silently thanking him.

He winked at her in reply.

Definitely less family resemblance than more, she decided.

Chapter Six

Janice drove him to an area in Anaheim known among contractors as tile row. As far as the eye could see was store after endless store offering every kind of tile.

She had just assumed the lead since this encompassed her territory. But the short journey across the freeway, for once not hopelessly congested, had her re-thinking her decision. Zabelle sat beside her now, wrapped in silence since she'd announced, "I'll drive," and gestured him into the passenger seat of her truck.

It wasn't the kind of comfortable silence of two old friends who momentarily had run out of things to say. This was the kind of silence bound up by tension. At least, for her it was.

As she got off the freeway and turned down the first of the streets leading to their destination, Janice felt she couldn't take the oppressive silence any longer.

"Anything wrong?" she asked. When Zabelle didn't answer, she repeated the question, her voice more forceful. This time, she managed to penetrate the haze.

"Hmm? Oh, no." And then Philippe looked at her for a moment before changing his reply. "Well, yes."

The light was red. "All right, what is it?"

Since she'd asked, he gave her an honest answer. "I'm not used to sitting in the passenger seat."

Janice wasn't sure she followed him. "Excuse me?"

"I'm usually the one driving."

Funny, if asked, she wouldn't have said he had an ego thing going. Apparently she was getting to be a worse judge of character than she thought. "But you don't know where we're going," she pointed out.

"I understand that," Philippe answered. "It's just that I guess I'm not comfortable having anyone else behind the wheel."

Well, that was pretty honest, she thought. Most men would have said something about being natural path-finders and being the better driver right out of the box. "I'm a safe driver," she told him.

He shook his head. "It's not that."

Making a left turn, she kept her eyes on the road. "You like being in control," she guessed.

That sounded obsessive, Philippe thought and he'd

never pictured himself that way. His mother had elements of obsessive-compulsive in her makeup, not him.

"No." The denial didn't taste quite right on his lips. And if he were being completely honest, if only with himself, maybe there was this one small streak that leaned toward control. "Well, maybe," he allowed, adding, "to some degree."

Janice had a feeling it was more than just that, but she wasn't about to push. Besides, they'd arrived at the first shop. She'd never come here herself, but some of the other contractors told her that the store had some very decent inventory.

"Lucky for you, we're here." With a smooth turn of her wrist, she pulled into what she believed would be the first of many parking lots that afternoon.

Instead of bolting out of the truck the way she'd expected him to, Zabelle sat on his side, eyeing the front of the store. The sign advertising the place was made completely out of black onyx. There were no windows in front. "This is the place?"

She got out, closing the door with finality, hoping that he'd take the hint. "This is one of them."

"One of them," he repeated. Slowly, without taking his eyes off the store, he got out of the truck. "How many are you planning on going to?"

She could almost hear him saying *dragging me to* in place of the words he'd used. "As many as it takes for you to find something you like." She gestured toward the other stores that lined both sides of the street. "I've never actually counted, but there are probably at least thirty or so stores along here."

"Thirty," he repeated incredulously.

"Or so," she added as a reminder.

Philippe slowly let out a long breath, as if bracing himself for an ordeal. He then squared his shoulders like a man going into battle and opened the front door. Stepping to the side, he held it for her, then glanced at her with a silent query.

For once, she could read him. "Don't worry, I'm not going to bite your head off for holding the door for me. I actually like that kind of thing."

Philippe responded to the warm smile on her lips. Given the line of work she was in, he wasn't sure if holding a door for her would somehow offend her sense of independence. Life in his mother's world had taught him to take nothing for granted about women's reactions to things.

"Good to know," he murmured.

The store looked deceptively small on the outside. Inside it was divided into fifteen or so sections, each showcasing a different kind of tile intended for every single foot of the house. Tile for the fireplace, for the pool area, for bathrooms, the kitchen and so on. There was so much to see that it was overwhelming.

Standing to the side, Janice could see that this was definitely a great deal more than Philippe had expected. Time for her to step in and be the tour guide, she thought.

Once she got started, she had a tendency to talk fast. This time Janice deliberately curbed her impulse. "I know that this can be a little mind-boggling at first. There are different grades of marble and granite, ceramic and glass—"

He seemed not to be listening. And then, just as she got warmed up to her subject, he pointed to a royal blue piece. "That one."

Janice blinked, and then looked at it. "That one what?"

"I pick that one. For the tile," he added since she was still staring at him as if he'd lapsed into an unknown dialect of pig Latin. "You can use that one for the tile." He glanced toward the door like a prisoner looking longingly at the gates leading to the freedom that was denied to him. "Can we go now?"

Janice remained speechless for exactly ten seconds before she regained possession of her tongue. "No, we can't go now," she answered in a tone she might have used on Kelli if she'd had a willful child instead of the one she'd been blessed with. "This is only the first place we've been to, Philippe, and just the first display you've seen. You have no idea what's out there," she insisted. "You might see something you like better."

It occurred to him, after the fact, that this was the first time she'd addressed him by his first name. It made the whole process seem more intimate somehow, like going out with a friend instead of an employee.

The thought had come shooting out of nowhere. He sent

it back to the same place. He was here to get this tile thing over with, not challenge himself with mental puzzles.

"I don't think so," he countered. He believed that it was entirely possible to find something he liked immediately instead of having to wade through a sea of candidates. "I don't have to see every single piece of tile to know what I like."

She'd bet anything that Zabelle was doing this because he didn't want to waste time going from store to store. Another contractor would have gone along with this, happy to have the ordeal over with. But she didn't operate that way. She liked leaving her clients satisfied with their renovations. That was what it was all about to her, matching the person to the changes, not just slapping any old thing together in order to collect her fee.

"I don't—" Janice got no further.

"If I were my mother," Philippe continued patiently, "you might have to wait six months for a decision. But I'm not like that."

Something else was going on here, she thought. But as of yet, she didn't have a clue so she could only tilt with the windmill she saw. "You can't go with the first tile you see."

"Why not?"

"Because there's so much out there that you haven't seen, that you don't know about, that you might really fall in love with," she added with feeling.

He looked at her for a long moment. So long that she

felt something inside her tighten in anticipation, although she hadn't a clue what it was.

And then, whatever it was that was going on, lessened and he said, "That sounds like my mother's philosophy about men."

She felt a little like someone who had just stepped in through the looking glass. "Excuse me?"

Ordinarily, he wouldn't have said that. Of the three of them, he was the most closed-mouth of Lily's sons. But somehow, around this little dynamo, words just seemed to slip out. "She moves from relationship to relationship, never staying long even if she falls in love." Especially when she falls in love, he added silently.

For the moment, Janice forgot about the tile. This was more interesting. "Why?"

It seemed ironic that his mother's reasoning seemed to align itself so readily with what J.D. had said about tile. "Because she feels that maybe she's settling, that maybe there's something even more spectacular out there and she's missing out." He raised his eyes to hers. "This one," he repeated. "I'll take this one."

So in some odd way, he was rebelling from behavior he'd witnessed as a child, she thought. Rebelling or not, she didn't want his bathrooms to suffer.

"You're sure you're not settling?" she prodded. An odd look came into his eyes, but she pushed forward. "Look, I realize that you're not marrying the tile, I just want you to like the finished product."

"I already told you, I like it. You can order however much you need. Can we go home now?" He repeated the question as if this time around it was rhetorical.

Philippe was surprised when she gave him an answer that was different from the one he'd assumed he would be receiving.

"No."

"No?" he echoed incredulously. How could the answer be no? "But I just did what you wanted," Philippe pointed out. "I picked a tile."

This was definitely not going to be her easiest assignment, despite the fact that the man claimed to be easy to please. She didn't want this to be something to get over with, she wanted it to leave a lasting impression on him, to catch his eye and dazzle him every time he walked into one of the bathrooms—or the kitchen for that matter.

"For the bathroom," she told him. "I won't go with the obvious, that there are three bathrooms to be remodeled—"

He cut in with a wave of his hand. "Same tile for all of them."

Janice pushed forward, pretending she hadn't heard that. "You still have to choose a slab for the kitchen counter, a backsplash, tile for all the floors, cabinets for the kitchen and bathrooms, fixtures, a tub for one, showers for the other two—"

"Wait," he cried, raising his hands as if he were

physically trying to stuff a profusion of things back into a box that had exploded before him, a box that was *not* allowing him to repack it. "Wait."

Temporarily out of steam, she paused to take a breath. "Yes?"

"What the hell is a backsplash?"

She grinned. "It's the area of the wall that runs along the back of the—"

His hand was up again, dismissing the explanation before it was completed. There was a bigger issue here. "I have to pick all those things out?"

"Well, yes." She'd shown him the blueprints. Hadn't any of this registered? Exactly how did he think this was all going to happen? "Oh, plus appliances for the kitchen."

Philippe stared at her, trying to process what she was saying and what it would cost him, not in the monetary sense but in man-hours. The latter was in short supply and he couldn't really spare what he did have available to him. At the outset, when he'd agreed to come with her, he'd expected the whole ordeal to last maybe an hour. Less if he could hurry her along. But what she was proposing would take days, days he didn't have.

This wasn't going to work out.

His first impulse was to tell her he'd changed his mind about having the rooms remodeled and pay her whatever penalty went with terminating the contract between them. An alternate plan was to postpone the work indefinitely, or at least until his own work was finished. Debating between them, he did neither.

For the same reason.

Instinct told him that J. D. Wyatt needed the money this job would bring in. So he chose another course, one that made complete sense to him. "You do it."

He couldn't mean what she thought me meant. "Excuse me?"

"You do it," he repeated.

A couple had come in with two children, the older of whom seemed to be around three and in excellent voice. He was exercising the latter and could be heard emitting a high-pitched scream from the far end of the store.

Unable to hear what Philippe was saying, Janice moved closer to her client. "Do what?"

"Pick for me," he told her simply.

"You want me to pick out your appliances." It wasn't a question so much as a stunned repetition.

"Yes. And all those other things you mentioned, too," he added.

"You have no idea what my taste is like."

He shrugged, fingering the tile he'd just selected and nodding at it as if it was privy to his thoughts. "Match it to my taste."

It took everything for her not to throw up her hands. Was he being difficult on purpose? "I don't know what your taste is like," she protested with feeling. "Other than bland."

He grinned, the corner of his eyes crinkling. "There you go."

Again, something stirred inside her, responding to the man and the moment. *Stop that,* she upbraided herself silently. "The idea is to get away from bland," she reminded him.

"I've got a contract deadline that I'm not going to make if I'm standing here in a tile store. Now it's either my way or we postpone this until I have some free time."

And that wouldn't be until November, based on what he'd said earlier. The easiest thing was to do as he said. But doing what he suggested went against her grain. Stuck, she thought for a second.

"How about this. I bring you samples and pictures of the things I picked out." She'd make sure he had a selection to choose from. She didn't mind being the go-between. It took longer, but that was part of her job and came under a heading related to hand-holding.

The thought of holding his hand created a warm wave inside her and increased her pulse rate.

Janice pushed it down and moved on. "That way you at least know you don't hate my choices."

"Sounds like a plan." He would have agreed to anything that would get him out of the store and on his way home again.

"May I help you?"

A salesman materialized behind them. Happy to see

someone he assumed would bring this all to an end, Philippe pointed to the royal blue ceramic tile he'd initially selected. "We want that tile."

The man beamed as he nodded. "Excellent choice, sir." Philippe had a feeling the man would have declared his selection "excellent" even if he had chosen something out of chewing gum. "And how much tile will you be requiring?"

Philippe shoved his hands into the front pockets of his jeans. "J.D., you're on." He gave every indication of retreating.

"That's what I like to see," the salesman declared. "A husband who lets his wife make the decisions. I'm sure you've done your homework, little lady."

Philippe stopped retreating. He didn't have to be his mother's son to know that J.D. had to find that tone offensive. He slanted a glance toward her, waiting to see her reaction.

"I have," she replied gamely, giving no indication that she would have enjoyed giving the man a swift kick for his patronizing manner. "And I'm not his wife, I'm his contractor."

The clerk seemed taken aback for a moment, but then, to his credit, he rallied. "Even better."

She was tempted to ask him why just to hear his answer. But that would be argumentative and she just wanted to move on, for Zabelle's sake. So instead, she put out her hand.

"Let me have your card," she requested easily. "We're not quite ready to order yet. I need to take some measurements first and then I'll get back to you."

It was obvious that the man felt once they were out the door, he stood a good chance of losing the sale. "We could have one of our men come by, double-check the numbers—"

"Won't be necessary," Janice assured him with a wide smile. Taking Philippe's arm, she hustled him out of the store and into the parking lot.

Bemused, Philippe looked at her as the door closed behind them. "Correct me if I'm wrong, but I thought you already had the measurements."

So he did pay attention, she thought. She inclined her head. "I do."

"Then why all that double-talk back there?" Although he had a feeling he already had the answer.

She led the way to her truck, intent on a quick getaway in case the salesman decided to follow them out to the parking lot out to make one last pitch. "I didn't like his attitude."

He struggled to keep his mouth from curving. "Is attitude that important?"

"It is in my line of work." She unlocked the truck from her side. The double click indicated that his side was open, too. "Don't worry, I saw who the manufacturer was. We can order that tile from any one of the stores I deal with on a regular basis," she promised. About to get in, she saw that he was still standing outside the passenger side. She took a guess. "You want to drive?"

That wasn't why he waited. He was watching the way a sunbeam was glinting in her hair, turning it a light shade of gold.

"No."

She thought he was just embarrassed because he was behaving so predictably. Rounding the hood, she came to his side.

"Go ahead," she urged, holding out the keys to him. "We're not going that far." The next store was only a few yards away.

After a moment's hesitation, he took the keys from her and crossed to the driver's side. Getting in, he asked, "Where's your favorite place to order tile?"

There were a couple of places she liked to frequent. Both were more than fair in price and reliability. Because there was so much competition, she liked to send business their way whenever possible.

She chose the one closest to where they were. "Orlando's. It's about a mile up the road."

"Good." Putting the key in the ignition, he started up the truck. "We'll go there."

She smiled to herself, shaking her head as she buckled up. "You just want to get this over with."

"Not that I don't find the company pleasing," he qualified, "but yes, I do."

Well, the man certainly didn't believe in beating

around the bush. And she could sympathize with deadlines and the need to get a project done by a specified time; when she'd worked for her father's company and dealt with major businesses, there'd been penalties for going over the allotted time.

She wondered if that applied to his work as well. "Make a left out of the lot," she instructed, pointing to the open road.

"Yes, ma'am."

In the end, they went with the tile he'd first selected. But not before she managed to get him to look at a few other pieces. She convinced him to get something slightly different for each of the three bathrooms. And just before they left the store, he'd wound up picking out the material for the kitchen counter: an impressive slab of granite known as blue pearl. It was almost black with veins of glimmering blue throughout.

"Damn," he murmured, a little stunned as he automatically got in behind the wheel more than an hour later. "I had no idea that there were that many different kinds of tile." She laughed and he caught himself thinking that it was a very peaceful yet arousing sound. "What?"

Her laughter had entered her eyes. "You didn't even begin to scratch the surface," she told him.

Philippe looked at her, a little stunned, wondering if that applied to her as well.

Chapter Seven

The noise didn't register until after the fact.

Somewhere, a door had closed. Someone was in the house. The next moment, he didn't have to speculate if it was one of his brothers.

One other person had the key to his house and it was that voice he heard now. Low and full-bodied like brandy being poured over ice, it filled the air, preceding her and coming at him without so much as a greeting or a preamble.

"And what is this I hear about you having the house remodeled?"

He glanced up from his computer to see her standing

in his doorway. Lily Moreau was given to dramatic entrances, even with her own family. By all accounts, she was a dramatic woman. From the top of her deep black hair, shot through with captivating streaks of gray, to the tips of her toes, polished, manicured and encased in the Italian designer shoes she favored, Lily Moreau, renowned artist, woman of passion and world traveler was the very personification of drama.

His smile was automatic. She was probably the most trying, infuriating woman in the world—she was at least in the top five—but he loved her dearly. "Hello, Mother, how are you?"

She took possession of the room and moved around like a force of nature, searching for a place to touch down, however briefly. Swirls of turquoise, at her wrists, ears and neck and along her torso, marked her path. Turquoise was one of her two favorite colors.

"Confused," she responded, pivoting to face him on the three-inch heels that rendered her five-foot-five. "My firstborn, the most stable child of the litter, has ventured into my territory without so much as a single request for input." She flounced down on the sofa, clouds of turquoise floating about her still trim hips and softly coming to rest in a circle around her. "I'd say I was more than confused. I'd say I was hurt."

Accustomed to these performances whenever his mother was in town, Philippe hardly looked away from his monitor and the equation that troubled him. "No reason to be hurt, Mother. And as for your 'territory,' since when have you been moonlighting as a handyman?"

"Handyman?" Frowning, Lily moved forward on the sofa. "I thought you were having the house redone." Although she strongly maintained that of the three of them, Philippe had inherited her artistic bent, he had always been determined to bury it. By now his flair was so far from the surface, it would have taken a crane to be resurrected. She liked being consulted on matters, liked being in the thick of things. Color schemes, textures, room dynamics, these all came under her purview.

"Not quite." He had a strong hunch he knew where his mother had gotten her information. Georges had been the one to let J.D. in the other day when she had dragged him off to those damn stores. "Tell Georges to get his facts straight."

"It wasn't Georges," she informed him, on her feet again and moving about. She stopped to finger a plant she had given him the last time she'd visited. It was two steps removed from death. On an errand of mercy, she walked into the hall, her destination the kitchen. "It was Alain."

"Tell Alain to get his facts straight next time," he called after her.

Philippe didn't bother asking how his other brother had gotten into this. He imagined it was like the old fashioned game of telephone, where Georges had taken his own interpretation of the events and told them to Alain who then put his own spin on it before telling their mother. He was actually surprised they didn't have him buying a villa in the south of France or some equally improbable scenario.

She was back with a cup full of water. Lily poured it slowly into the pot, then tried to arrange the drooping, drying leaves. "And the facts are?"

Philippe glanced at his mother. He should have known that she would want in on this. She was the one he should have sent with J.D., not gotten roped into traipsing around after the woman from store to store, selecting things that held little to no interest for him. All he'd wanted was to have a cracked sink replaced.

But to say anything on that subject would get him sucked into a conversation he didn't want. "That you don't come by enough for me to see you with a scowl on your face."

"Scowl?" The plant was completely forgotten. Lily reached for her purse and the compact mirror inside. "I'm scowling? I can't scowl, I'll get wrinkles before my big show." Mirror opened, she reviewed her appearance from several different angles, then decided that she was fine. Not twenty-two-year-old fine, but fine nonetheless.

Philippe caught the magic word. "Another big show?"

"Always another big show," she declared with gusto. It was what she thrived on, that and the men in her life. "If I can't paint, I'll just lie down and they can throw dirt over me." She tossed her head, dark ends flirting with the tops of her shoulders. "I'll be as good as dead."

She certainly had a way of phrasing things, he thought. "They throw enough dirt over you, you will be." One of the first things he'd ever learned about his mother was that, barring some crisis, there was nothing she liked to talk about more than her paintings, so he gave her a gentle nudge in that direction. "So, where and when is this big show?"

"Three weeks from Saturday at the Sunset Galleries on Lido Isle." She recited the information as if it had been prerecorded. And then she gave him a deep, pene-trating look. "You'll be there?"

Turning in his chair so that he faced her instead of the computer, he grinned. "Wouldn't miss it."

She took hold of his hands as if that was all she needed to discern whether or not he was telling her the truth. Fingers wound tightly around his palms.

"No, really, you'll be there?" She nodded absently toward the screen. "You know how you get when you get involved in your work."

"I'll be there," he promised, wiping any trace of a smile from either his voice or his face.

Lily sighed, as if getting him to agree had been an ordeal. "Good. I want you to meet him."

"Him?" Philippe eyed his mother warily. "There's another *him?*" He should have known there would be. It had been, what, five months since the last one had been sent packing? That was a long dry spell for his mother.

"Yes," Lily replied joyously. She'd moved on to the

rear of the room to gaze out at the backyard it faced. All three houses shared it as if it was one large yard instead of the culmination of three. "You need a gazebo, Philippe," she decided and then, glancing back at him, she waved her hand. "Get that look off your face, I know what you're thinking."

He made it a point to be as laid-back as she was dramatic. "I sincerely doubt that."

She was not his mother for nothing. "You're thinking, *here we go again.*"

He laughed, impressed. "Very good. I guess I'm getting too predictable."

She didn't waste words on defending her past choices. She was a woman who had always believed in moving forward. "This time, it's different."

And where had he heard that before? Philippe mused. He went back to focusing on his work, uttering a tolerant, "Of course it is."

"It is," she insisted, crossing to his desk and presenting herself behind his monitor so that he was forced to look at her. She clasped her hands together and resembled a schoolgirl in the throes of her first major crush. "Kyle is everything I've been looking for in a man. Funny, smart, youthful and vigorous—"

Philippe shot his hand up in the air to halt the flow of words. "If that word doesn't apply to the way he polishes your silverware, Mother, I really don't want to hear about it."

Lily rolled her eyes. "Oh Philippe, you know what your trouble is?"

Yes, he had a mother who had never grown up. "I'm sure you'll tell me," he replied patiently.

She took his chin in her hand, lowering her face to his. "You're not at all like your father."

Moving his chair back, he eyed his mother. "I thought that was a good thing. You left my father because he gambled away the floor from under your feet," he reminded her.

She refused to dwell on the bad. It was one of her attributes. "But first he swept me off those feet, Philippe. He had this zest for life—"

"Otherwise known as Texas hold 'em."

"Oh Philippe," she sighed mightily, "you were born old."

He didn't see it as a failing. If anything, it kept him from making his mother's mistakes and leading with his heart instead of his head. "One of us had to be and someone had to be there for the boys."

The hurricane stopped moving. Lily's expression turned serious. "Was having me as a mother so terrible?"

He wouldn't allow his mind to stray to the hundred and one shortcomings his mother possessed. The bottom line was that she meant well in her own way and she did love them. Of that he was certain. So he smiled at her and said, "You had your moments."

"I had my hours, Philippe, my days," she corrected majestically. "And I always loved all you boys to distraction." Long, slender fingers touched his cheek the way she did when he was small and needed her comforting. "I still do."

"I know that."

She dropped her hand to her side. The movement was accompanied by the sound of gold bracelets greeting one another. "I'm a passionate woman, Philippe. I need passion for my art. I *use* passion," she insisted.

This was a conversation they'd had before. Several times. "I know that, too, Mother."

She kissed his cheek, then rubbed away the streak of vivid red from his skin. Any minor disagreement that might have arisen was terminated before it had a chance to form. "Is there a reason for this handiwork you're having done?"

"Yes," he replied simply, "the bathroom sink is cracked."

"Oh." She looked exceptionally disappointed. "I was hoping that it was being done because you were finally settling down."

Philippe addressed the phrase in its strictest sense. "I'm the most *settled* out of the three of us," he reminded her.

The drama returned as Lily sighed and resumed her restless patrol of the small converted bedroom. "With a woman, Philippe, settling down with a woman." She retraced her steps and presented herself before him again. "Have you been seeing anyone?"

"Only you when I'm lucky."

Lily closed her eyes and sighed. "Use that charm on someone else, Philippe. Someone who matters."

Momentarily surrendering, he rose to his feet. He just wasn't going to get any work done with his mother here, bombarding him with questions. He might as well enjoy this visit.

"You always matter, Mother. Want some coffee?" he suggested.

She looked as if she was going to say yes, then surprised him by shaking her head.

"I don't want to take you away from what you're doing." She took exactly one step toward the threshold before she continued talking. "Just wanted to invite you to the show and to see if you had any women stashed here." The expression on her face told him that she hoped he'd do better on her next unexpected visit. "Your father always had women stashed here and there."

There wasn't very much he remembered about his parents' union when it had been official, although his mother had taken his father back for a short time between her second and third husbands. But they hadn't been married then. "Before you got engaged?"

Lily moved a stray hair from her cheek. "No, after we were married. After gambling and family, women were your father's primary addiction." She said it matter-of-factly, as if it had no impact on her what-soever. Lily might have been a cauldron of emotion, but she was never judgmental.

Philippe blew out a breath. "Not much of a prize," he commented.

But his mother's eyes were shining like two bright jewels. "Vigorous, Philippe. He, too, was very vigorous."

It was going to take him days to get the image she'd planted out of his head, Philippe thought. If he were still at a young and impressionable age, that just might have scarred him for life.

But then, if his mother's actual lifestyle hadn't done it while he was growing up, he sincerely doubted that anything at this stage possibly could. Flamboyant, ec-centric and completely unorthodox were all terms that were synonymous with the name Lily Moreau and he'd survived his childhood to become a relatively well-adjusted, successful man. If his house was a little empty at times, well, everyone paid some kind of price in life. Being alone was his.

Besides, it was a great deal more preferable than constantly making the wrong choices.

His mother still hovered over him. "I worry about you most of all, Philippe."

That was the last thing he wanted. For her to worry or, worse, to do something about that worry.

He had only one response for that. "Don't."

She sniffed, taking offense. "I may not be Norman

Rockwell's idea of the perfect mother, but I'm still a mother."

He knew she meant well. Philippe softened. "Norman Rockwell's been gone for a long time, I don't think you need to worry about him. And I appreciate the concern, Mother, but I am a grown man. We march to different drummers. You taught me that, remember?"

"Yes, but sometimes the music is the same." She pressed full lips together, thinking. And then her eyes widened the way they did when she'd been struck by an idea she liked. "Kyle has a sister—"

For a second, the name escaped him. "Kyle?"

"Yes, the reason for the smile on my face. You're not paying attention, Philippe," she admonished with a trace of impatience.

His mother's boyfriend's sister. Oh God. That was all he needed, to be coupled with a woman old enough to be his mother. That little tidbit would finally send him into therapy.

He put his hands on her shoulders, as if that could somehow push all the wild ideas she had back into her head. "Mother," his tone was firm, "Don't worry about it. Now, I do have work to do, so…"

She took her dismissal graciously enough and picked up the purse she'd dropped onto the sofa upon entry. "I'll let myself out, I know the way." She hesitated for a second. "You won't forget about the show?"

"I won't forget."

She nodded, taking him at his word. "And see if you can bring someone," she coaxed, then added with emphasis, "Someone female."

"I'll see what I can find on Amazon.com," he deadpanned.

Lily sighed. "Some things never change." Raising herself up on her toes, she kissed his cheek again. "But I love you anyway."

He smiled as she left the room. "Nice to know, Mother."

Sitting down, within moments Philippe was lost again in the details of the knotty programming problem he'd run up against.

And then he was roused out of its midst again.

"Philippe?"

He closed his eyes, summoning strength. He didn't often get impatient with his mother, there was no point. But he could get impatient at the loss of an afternoon's work, especially since he'd sacrificed an afternoon just the other day.

Taking a deep breath, he released it again before saying, "Yes, Mother?"

"You are a sneaky devil."

The single sentence, hanging in the air without preamble, begged for questions, for an explanation. He pushed away from his desk and rose to his feet, resigned to getting both.

"Why, Mother?"

There was no answer. He was about to follow the

sound of his mother's voice when the need was abruptly vanquished. Lily made a reentrance.

She wasn't alone.

His mother's ring-encrusted fingers were delicately wrapped around the small hand of J.D.'s daughter. J.D. was right behind them, bringing up the rear.

Philippe felt like the beach at Normandy on D-day.

"Where have you been hiding these two?" his mother asked with the air of someone who felt she had the right to know everything that transpired in the world of her sons.

"We're not hiding," Kelli informed her before he could find his own tongue. "We're right here."

J.D. seemed a little overwhelmed by his mother. Welcome to the club, he thought.

"Did we have a date I forgot about?" he asked. The second the word was out of his mouth, he realized his mistake. His colossal mistake.

"Date?" Lily echoed, vibrating with both curiosity and joy.

"I came for the check," J.D. explained. She was sure she'd mentioned it to him.

Lily's eyes widened. "He's paying you? Oh, Philippe—"

Janice had no idea what was going on but she just pushed ahead, hoping that somehow everything would straighten itself out if she just hung on to her part of the truth. "I didn't think you'd mind if I brought Kelli with me again." She tried to take Kelli's hand, but the woman in turquoise was in her way. "She really wanted to see you."

"He is charming, my son," Lily agreed and turned to the woman she assumed was the child's mother. "I'm Lily Moreau. It's very nice to meet you."

The next thing Janice knew, she found herself enfolded in an enthusiastic one-armed hug. Although she hugged Kelli at every opportunity, she came from a family that was light-years removed from anything demonstrative. She wasn't sure how to respond to this strange woman's embrace.

"Likewise," she murmured from within the embrace.

Letting go, Lily turned to her son again. "Philippe, out with it. Who is this lovely creature?"

"She's my contractor, Mother."

Lily laughed dryly. "You have your father's sense of humor. I would find him alone with all sorts of beautiful women. He always referred to them as his clients. Even in the dead of night when I came back from a tour and discovered him indisposed, so to speak." There was no malice, no hurt in her voice. She was simply recounting something from the past that had occurred in her life.

Still, Philippe couldn't believe she was saying this in front of a stranger. "Mother," he said sharply, glancing at J.D.

"I really am his contractor," Janice told her. "I need a check from you to make a down payment on the materials we decided on," she told him.

Kelli tugged on the woman's hand. "I'm Kelli," she informed her. And then proceeded to blow her away by asking, "Are you the lady who painted the pretty picture over there?"

Lily seemed stunned and then immensely pleased. "Why, yes, I am." She bent down to Kelli's level. "Do you like it?"

Kelli's hair bounced about her face as she nodded. "Very much." And then she added in a very grown-up voice, "I paint, too."

Lily smiled warmly. "Do you, now?" There was genuine interest in her voice, not just the sound of forced tolerance.

"Yes, she does. Very well."

The confirmation with its comment came not from Kelli or even J.D., but from Philippe. His mother looked at him with an interested expression that immediately told him he should have kept that comment to himself.

But since he hadn't, he might as well back up what he'd said. He looked at J.D. "Why don't you show my mother the drawing you carry around with you?"

Janice paused. It was one thing to show the drawing to a person she was talking to, it was another to show it to a woman who had had her paintings on display in galleries in Paris.

But Kelli gazed up at her so eagerly, there was nothing else she could do. Taking out her wallet, Janice carefully unfolded the drawing she kept tucked away there, then handed it to Lily.

Lily studied the drawing with great interest. "You did this?" There wasn't a hint of a patronization in her voice.

Kelli nodded. "Uh-huh."

Lily's smile crinkled into her eyes. "Really?"

"Really," Kelli echoed, then crossed her heart with childish fingers.

Lily looked up in Janice's direction. "This is very, very good."

Janice already knew that, but it was nice to hear a professional agree. "Thank you."

Lily studied the drawing again. It looked better to her with each pass. "Have you thought of getting your daughter some professional training?"

It was one of her cherished hopes, but it was something to address in the future, not now. "She's a little young for that."

"How old is she?" Lily asked.

Kelli responded instantly. "I'm four and three-quarters."

"Oh, four and three-quarters," Lily parroted, suppressing a smile. She glanced up at Janice. "Mozart was four when he wrote his first concerto."

"Well, he ultimately didn't wind up very well, did he?" Janice countered. She didn't want anyone treating Kelli like some oddity.

"Well-read, too." Lily nodded, looking back at her

son. Her comment, clearly about J.D., was for Philippe's benefit. "You've given me hope, Philippe."

"Remodeling, Mother, she's remodeling a couple of rooms for me."

"Four," Janice corrected. "I'm remodeling four rooms for you."

"Very promising," Lily commented. Philippe could almost see his mother's thoughts racing off to the finish line. Any protest he might offer would only make the woman believe the very opposite. This was a case of discretion being the better part of valor.

So for the time being, he kept his silence and hoped for the best. He'd survived Hurricane Lily before.

Chapter Eight

Like most people, Philippe had a temper. However, unless one of his own was being threatened, it took a great deal to nudge that particular part of his personality awake. He usually took things in stride. Being stuck in bumper-to-bumper traffic didn't faze him. But deadlines that came and went, *his* deadlines, made him uneasy. Because he felt responsible for the failure to meet this particular deadline, he'd become progressively more irritated.

And God knew, the noise wasn't helping.

Philippe looked accusingly at the closed door. He'd been in his office for the last three hours and it was just getting worse.

This was definitely not what he had bargained for.

Afraid of losing his work, he saved it, assigning the program's temporary name yet another number to differentiate it from previous versions. He laced his fingers together behind his head and leaned back in his chair.

When he'd agreed to have work done on his house, he'd forgotten to consider one important thing.

The noise factor.

Right now, the house abounded with it. How could one woman create this much noise? It seeped into every crevice of the house, taking his office prisoner.

It didn't matter if his door was open or closed. He was still very much aware of it. Sometimes the noise was loud, sometimes almost deceptively soft, making him think that perhaps he'd weathered the worst. But then it would start again. And continue.

At its best, the noise could be likened to an erratic heartbeat. At its worst, it was like the circus setting up winter quarters outside his door—with a herd of less-than-tame elephants in charge of doing all of the hammering.

It had been like this for three days.

Philippe dragged his fingers through his hair and counted to ten. And then ten again. It didn't help. His long dormant temper had gone short-fuse on him.

Abandoning his computer and its multitude of crashes, Philippe went out into the hallway and made his way to the kitchen, the source of all this ungodly noise.

He was ready to do whatever it took to get some peace.

Wearing safety goggles and wielding a sledgehammer, J.D. didn't seem to see him at first. For a second, despite the irritation that was close to the boiling point within his chest, he hung back, just watching her.

She swung that sledgehammer like a pro. Tirelessly. Splintering cabinets she'd already crowbarred from the wall.

He found the rhythmic movement oddly hypnotic. J.D. wore faded jeans that seemed to lovingly adhere to her every curve and a gray T-shirt that was damp in several places, obviously with her sweat.

Construction had never looked so good.

Something inside him stirred as he continued to watch her work.

One final swing and she broke apart the last of the cabinets. Now the mess just needed to be hauled away. The kitchen was gutted, barren, like the aftermath of a hurricane. He assumed the rebuilding would begin tomorrow. He'd never gotten around to picking out his new appliances. He'd left that entirely up to J.D. A small part of him couldn't help wondering if perhaps that had been a mistake.

She had muscles, he realized as he stared at the way they moved and flexed.

Damn, he was turned on. What was that all about? Yes, she was an attractive woman, but this went beyond just acknowledgement of that fact.

He was working too hard, he told himself. And his brain was tired.

Janice sensed his presence a moment before she retired the sledgehammer. Every single muscle in her body ached from exhaustion. One more swing and she would have dropped the hammer. Her hands couldn't hold on to the handle for another second.

She glanced up in his direction just as she wiped more perspiration from her brow with the back of her wrist. He was looking at the rubble.

"Pretty awful, isn't it?" she commented, guessing at what had to be going through his brain. Right about now, Zabelle probably couldn't envision that this chaos would, in the end, give way to something really nice.

Philippe nodded. "Yeah, that's why I'm here."

She didn't follow him and wondered if eccentricity ran in the family. His mother had all but commandeered her last week when they'd first met, absorbing much of her afternoon. The woman seemed absolutely taken with her daughter and since both Kelli and Lily shared a love of art, she had seen that as a good thing.

But there was no denying that Lily Moreau was not your ordinary woman by any stretch of the imagination. She took getting used to. And indulging.

She wouldn't have said that about Philippe, but then, she really didn't know him that well. One prolonged shopping trip did not exactly make her privy to his soul.

"All right," Janice replied, drawing out the words and hoping that Philippe would fill in the blanks.

He picked up a kitchen towel that was tossed on the table. Rather than offer it to her, he wiped away the line of perspiration that had plastered her hair to her forehead.

His hand moved in short, sure strokes along her forehead.

Their eyes met. He took a breath, realizing that his brain had vacated the premises. "I think I made a mistake."

"On your work?" she guessed. Having him this close was scrambling her insides. Either that or there was a sudden lack of air in the room.

He moved his head slowly from side to side, still gazing into her eyes. They were almost a hypnotic blue, he thought. "On yours."

"You might find you need to write in code, but talking in it is wasted on me. You're going to have to explain what you just said."

He seemed surprised. Belatedly, he dropped his hand and the towel to his side. "You know about binary code?"

She didn't see what the big deal was. After all, it wasn't as if she'd just solved the space/time continuum problem.

"I've got three-quarters of a B.A.," she reminded him, although she really didn't expect him to remember. Her educational background had been on her résumé and references.

To her surprise, Philippe did remember. "I've been

meaning to ask you, how does someone get just three-quarters of a degree?"

That was a sore point for her, but one she needed to face. "You do it by dropping out in your senior year before taking any tests."

So near and yet so far, he thought, shaking his head. "If you were that close, why didn't you stay?" It made no sense to him. He went to lean against a counter and stopped himself just in time. Another second and he would have been sitting on the floor—beside the rubble she had created.

"Because I was going to be that big." Fingers almost touching, she held them out as far as she could before her very thin, very flat stomach. "I was pregnant at the time with Kelli."

"Why didn't you go back once she was born?"

She managed to hold at bay the sadness that always came whenever she thought of that period of her life. "Because by then, I was a widow and Kelli needed to live somewhere other than inside a cardboard box." She took a breath. This didn't have anything to do with the reason she was hired. She had no idea why she was playing true confessions with this man.

"Still, I think you should go back and get your degree."

"I intend to one day, when life gets a little more comfortable."

He wondered at her definition of *comfortable.* Philippe reminded himself of the reason he'd come in search of her and scanned the gutted room. From where he stood, it looked close to hopeless. "How much longer?"

She took off her gloves and flexed her hands. Her palms still ached from gripping the sledgehammer. "Until what?"

Philippe turned back to look at her. "Until you're done."

"With the kitchen?" She refrained from reminding him that everything had already been spelled out in the contract, including dates. She watched him shifting his weight from foot to foot. He seemed restless.

That made two of them.

"No, *done* done," he emphasized. "With everything," he added when she didn't answer.

Because she loved her job, Janice worked fast but there was only so much she could do alone. Besides, the job was dependent on other people as well, people who had to get back to her with the necessary items she ordered, like the rock quarry that was going to be delivering the granite slab Philippe had ordered. She couldn't move ahead and install the sink until the counter arrived. As for the maple cabinets she'd ordered for him, they were due at the beginning of next week. She crossed her fingers mentally, hoping he would approve of them.

"Well, barring any mishaps, if all conditions are a go, I'd say you could have your house back in as little as six to eight weeks."

Philippe shook his head. "That's not going to work."

Uh-oh, here comes trouble. Well, nothing in her life

had ever been easy, why start now? She drew herself up and challenged, "Why?"

"Because I can't work with all this noise. I thought I could, but I can't."

A lot of times, people moved into a hotel when she worked on their house. But he looked unreceptive when she made the suggestion. "You could try ear plugs," she told him. "Or you could try working when I knock off for the day."

So far, she'd arrived each morning at seven and left by three-thirty. He wasn't about to set his alarm for three in the morning to work before she arrived and then start again after she left.

He shook his head. "I do my best in the morning."

Janice smiled. So they had that in common. "So do I."

Philippe thought for a moment. "Can't you work any faster?"

"I could. If I were twins." She paused, thinking. There was a way, but it involved a complication. "I could get my brother to work with me."

As he recalled, she used her brother as a babysitter. "Does he do this kind of thing?"

"Yes." It was probably his imagination, but she seemed to answer the question a little too quickly, as if she didn't want to give herself any time to think about it.

"Then get him." He saw a hesitant look pass over her face. "What? If it's a matter of more money, I'm sure we can arrive at a figure that's mutually satisfying."

"No, it's not that." She'd quoted a price and she was going to stand by it. With Gordon helping, the job would get done faster so that balanced things out. "Gordon's my babysitter. If he's working here with me, I'm going to have to bring Kelli along as well, at least until I can find someone else."

It was a little unusual, but then, nothing about J. D. Wyatt was usual. "So?"

She looked at him for a long moment, trying to discern if he was pulling her leg. "You wouldn't mind?"

"No. She seemed like a nice enough, quiet little girl." He thought of Kelli's love for painting. "We could set something up for her in the family room—the part that hasn't been invaded with groceries, dishes and small appliances," he qualified.

"All right, then—" Janice began to pivot on her heel.

"But I'm just curious about one thing."

She stopped in her tracks, waiting for the shoe to drop. "Go ahead."

"Why isn't she in preschool, or nursery school, or whatever it is that they call it these days?"

Janice had her own philosophy about that. She believed that the first few years of life should be spent around the people who love you. She'd been farmed out when she was Kelli's age. Her father couldn't deal with raising children so she and Gordon had been sent off to day care and left with people before and after school. She'd always promised herself that her own child would be raised differently, that her daughter would never waste a single moment of her life wondering if her parents loved her.

"Kelli's going into kindergarten this fall. I just wanted to keep her around for as long as possible. She has friends on the block and there's nothing she could learn in preschool that I can't cover."

He nodded, getting the feeling that he'd intruded. "Fair enough." He regrouped. "All right then, why don't you knock it off for today and then come back tomorrow with reinforcements?"

"You're the boss." The tone she used had him sincerely doubting she believed that. "You going to go back in there and work now?" she guessed.

It was getting close to noon. "After I go out to get something to eat since you've taken away my stove." He looked at the barren area where his stove had once stood. She hadn't asked him for help, the way he'd assumed she would. "How did you manage that, anyway?"

"I used a dolly and a ramp and I walked it across the floor."

"How?"

She grinned. "You move each side one at a time. First right, then left, then right and so on until you're across the room."

He and his brothers had always subscribed to the brute force method. "How did you get it on the truck?" he asked.

That had been the simplest part. "I borrowed a friend's truck. He's got a hydraulic lift."

It made sense, he supposed. It still bothered him a little that she was so much more adept at this kind of thing than he was. "Answer for everything, eh?"

The wide smile on her lips took him aback for a minute, as did the churning sensation in his stomach that came in response. "Including your lunch."

"Come again?"

"I made you something." Thinking he'd remain in his office the way he had the other three days, she'd planned on surprising him and having the meal ready on the dining room table by noon. The best laid plans of mice and men...

He stared at her incredulously. "You cook for your clients?"

This was a first, but then, Kelli had taken such a shine to him and she did feel as if she were invading his space just a little.

But in response to his question, Janice shrugged. "I made lasagna last night. I always make too much so I thought I'd bring some over." She tossed him a smile over her shoulder as she walked out to her truck.

"But I don't have a stove," he reminded her.

"There's a microwave buried on the sofa somewhere. Besides, it's good cold," she promised, leaving the room.

He was still staring at the jumbled mess on his sofa, trying to make out the shape of the microwave, when J.D. returned a few minutes later, carrying what appeared to be a large, rectangular blue and white chest made of hard plastic. It look unwieldy and he moved to take it from her.

When he did, he discovered that it was more than unwieldy, it was heavy. "You're a lot stronger than you look," he told her, bringing the chest over to the dining room table.

"I have to be," she quipped.

Setting the box down on the table, he saw her raise one eyebrow in a silent question. "I've decided to have it cold."

"Translation." She laughed. "You can't locate the microwave."

"Beside the point," he declared nonchalantly. He had, however, located two plates and he had one at each place setting now. "Join me?"

She was surprised he asked. "I thought I was being dismissed."

He supposed he had sounded rather abrupt. But he hated being stumped and the program was driving him crazy. "Is that how it sounded?"

Taking her seat at his right, she noticed that Philippe hadn't actually apologized. "You have a very authoritative voice."

He laughed, taking a seat himself. "Comes from telling my brothers what to do."

"You were a fledgling bully?" she asked. Because the lasagna was hers, she did the honors, cutting portions.

"I was the father figure. Or, I should say," he

amended, "the *stable* father figure since there were an abundance of other father figures milling around most of the time." He stopped abruptly as his words echoed back to him. This wasn't like him. "Why am I always spilling my guts to you?"

Her smile was encouraging, understanding. "I have the kind of face people talk to. I'm more or less invisible," she explained. "They don't feel that they'll see me again once the job is over, but for the duration, they have invited me into their home and since I'm there, they come to regard me as someone they can talk to." She grinned, sinking her fork into the piece she'd taken. "I'm like the family pet without the emotional investment."

That definitely was *not* the way he saw her. "We never had a pet."

"Not even goldfish?"

He shook his head. "For a while, Mother traveled around too much for us to have pets. And then when she finally bought the house and we stayed behind while she went on her tours, she made it clear she didn't want anything with fur, feathers or fins finding its way to our mailing address." Because he felt that he'd said too much again, he changed the subject. He nodded at his plate. "This is good."

"Thank you." His compliment pleased her more than she thought it might. *Careful, J.D., you've slid down this path before and all you got for your trouble is skinned knees.* "I wouldn't have brought it if it was bad."

The reply tickled him. "So, what other talents do you have?"

She didn't have to stop to think. "That pretty much covers it."

In his estimation, that was more than enough. She cooked like a house afire and could build a replacement if the need arose. "You ever think about starting your own restaurant?"

Not even for a moment. "Ninety-five percent of all restaurants fail in their first year. I need a sure thing and working with these—" she held up her hands "—is a sure thing."

He could understand her reasoning, not that the world of contractors was all that stable. "Where did you learn to cook like this?"

"It was necessity." She paused to take a bite herself. "After my mother left, it was either learn to cook or eat ready-made things out of a box."

He curbed the desire to ask her about her mother. If she wanted him to know more, she'd tell him. As for preparing things out of a box, she'd just described the way he lived. "Nothing wrong with that."

"Have you read what they put inside that stuff?"

He shrugged, then swallowed what was in his mouth before answering, "Food."

"Food whose ingredients are guaranteed to give you high blood pressure and shut down your kidneys by the time you reach middle age." Turning, she reached into the blue and white box and took out a small round bowl. "I brought you fruit for dessert." She took off the cover. "Blueberries. They're rich in antioxidants."

He laughed, shaking his head as he looked at the offering. "Anyone ever tell you that you're pushy?"

"Maybe once or twice," she allowed.

He was willing to bet it was more than that.

Philippe glanced down at his plate. Somehow, he'd managed to eat the entire portion without realizing it. The blueberries, however, held no interest for him. He moved back from the table.

"Thanks, that was really good. But you don't have to do this, you know."

"I know." She gathered up the dirty dishes, putting them back into the chest.

Philippe started to offer to do them for her and then realized that he couldn't. She'd ripped out his sink that morning. With the chest between her hands, she began to make her way to the front door. He noticed that she was leaving her tools behind.

"Don't you need to take anything else with you?"

She glanced back at the toolbox. "Why? You're my only client."

He took the chest from her, indicating that he was going to follow her out with it. "I'm sorry to hear that."

"Why?"

"Well, it means that business is bad, right?"

She shook her head. "No, it means that I only do one

client at a time." She unlocked the door and took the chest from him, placing it behind the front seat of her truck. "I was serious about that. This way, it'll get done faster."

"And with your brother working with you, it'll be even that much faster."

She was going to have to keep after Gordon, she thought. He did good work—when he was working. But given half a chance, he'd take off for a few hours or catch a nap.

"Absolutely," she promised.

Ten minutes later, J.D. had left and he was back at his desk. His appetite appeased, his brain cleared, Philippe was in a much better frame of mind to take another crack at the program.

Bathed in absolute quiet, after a few minutes, Philippe realized that he found the silence almost deafening.

With a resigned sigh, he shook his head and turned on the radio to fill up the empty spaces.

Chapter Nine

Somewhere between the time his alarm sounded and he toweled himself dry from his shower, it hit Philippe like a bullet right between the eyes.

He was looking forward to seeing J.D. Looking forward to seeing her even with the accompanying wall of noise. The realization caught him off guard. He tried not to dwell on it, tried not to attach any sort of deep meaning to it. He didn't, by definition, dislike people and she was a person. The woman had turned out to be a decent sort, that was all. No big deal.

If it was no big deal, why did he feel compelled to convince himself of that? It should have just been a given.

Making a disgusted noise that drew into service a mangled French phrase, one of the few things he had learned from his father, he focused his mind on what was important. His work.

Philippe had forced himself up early, showering and shaving a good ninety minutes before he usually left the confines of his bed. With a stale piece of toast and marginal coffee, he sat before his computer, pondering the merit of a particular equation on his screen when he heard the doorbell.

Or thought he did.

It turned out to be a false alarm. Just his ears playing tricks on him.

There was no one at the door.

Glancing around, seeing only a jogger in the distance, Philippe experienced a smattering of disappointment. He retreated. Somehow, this was all wrong, although he couldn't begin to untangle the reasons why. He had work to do.

Maybe he was working too hard. Rather than take his time or kick back, as was his cousin Beau's habit, Philippe was always doggedly at his desk, working every available moment he had. Because he believed that all work and no play not only made Jack a dull boy but also helped contribute to the death of his brain cells, he had gone out of his way to institute his weekly poker game, making sure never to miss one.

But maybe that wasn't enough. Maybe, like his

mother had said to him time and again, he needed to get out of his shell. Needed to go out. With someone of the opposite gender.

Philippe frowned.

The fact that he was even thinking like this was proof that he needed to let up a little. To let go.

Right after this baby's packed up, he promised himself.

Famous last words, he mocked. He'd thought somewhere along the same lines when he'd worked on the last program—and all he'd done was jump right into this one.

Just before he reached his office threshold, Philippe stopped abruptly. Cocking his head to the right, he listened intently.

No, this time the doorbell wasn't his imagination. Retracing his steps back to the front door, he swung it open.

And smiled.

Kelli was clearly the one who had rung his doorbell. She was standing on her toes, stretching as far as she could, about to press her small finger to the white button again. When the door opened, she offered him a smile that he imagined angels looked to as a standard by which to measure their own smiles.

"I'm here," she announced brightly.

He exchanged looks with J.D. who was standing beside her. A man in jeans and a T-shirt was behind them. His wheat-colored hair and fair complexion fairly shouted that he was related to both.

"So I see," Philippe said, turning his attention back

to Kelli. He hadn't really intended to take the girl's hand, but Kelli had other ideas. She slipped her small hand into his and then tugged him back into his house.

"I brought stuff to do," she informed him. "So I won't get in your way."

How could someone so young sound so adult? He nodded in response. "Very thoughtful of you."

She beamed. Then suddenly, as if she'd forgotten her manners, she turned around to look at the man behind her. "This is my Uncle Gordon. Mama says you want your house done faster." A little pint-sized feminine pride slipped into her narrative. "Uncle Gordon is fast, but not as fast as Mama."

Philippe caught himself wondering just how fast Mama was. Reining in his thoughts, he slanted a glance toward J.D.

Damn, but worn T-shirts never looked so good to him before. "I'll bet," he acknowledged.

Something in his tone had Janice struggling to tamp down a wave of warmth. She raised her chin a little, not certain if she should be defensive or not.

But she could be polite. She nodded at her daughter, her eyes on Philippe's. "Thanks for letting me do this."

"No problem." He glanced at the man standing behind the little stick of dynamite who still had his hand. "I'm Philippe Zabelle." He extended his other hand to Kelli's uncle. "Nice to meet you."

Gordon was nothing if not friendly. Grinning

broadly, he shook the hand that was offered to him. "Yeah, likewise." Walking toward the kitchen, he looked around as he passed. "Nice place you have here."

Philippe's laugh was dismissive. "For a bomb shelter."

Gordon turned around. "No, I mean it. You've got a really great exterior." He jerked his thumb toward the front of the house. "It gives the place a ritzy look."

Philippe supposed so, but that had never been the draw for him. The fact that he and his brothers could all lead separate lives but still be in close proximity to one another was what had sold him on the house.

That, and that the fact that the outside was painted Wedgwood blue with white trim. Most of the other houses in the immediate vicinity were painted either in shades of rust or in some drab, strange color never to be found in nature. Blue had always been his favorite color.

The clock was ticking, Janice thought. Both for her and, probably more importantly, for Philippe. She broke up the impromptu meeting.

"C'mon, Kel, let's get you settled in," she said, taking the little girl's free hand. In her other hand, Janice was carrying a large portfolio filled with several drawings and a painting that Kelli was currently working on. Pausing, she eyed Philippe hesitantly. "It is all right that we use your dining room table, isn't it?" she asked, quickly adding, "I brought this tablecloth so that it doesn't accidentally get dirty."

"Actually," Philippe cut in, "I've got a much better idea."

Kelli watched him eagerly, a kernel of corn about to pop. Janice, hearing the same sentence, felt very protective of Kelli's feelings. She didn't want anything to diminish the girl's zest. "Such as?"

He led the way to an alcove just off the living room. Yesterday, there had been a refrigerator shoved into the space. He'd moved it last night to the already overflowing family room. He had something different in mind for the space.

"I thought Kelli might like to use something else instead of just a flat surface." Walking past the living room, he gestured over to the alcove. It was empty now—except for the small easel that stood in the center.

Kelli's eyes became huge. "Look, Mama, it's kid size," she exclaimed, running over to it. She touched the easel reverently, as if afraid it would disappear once her fingers came in contact with it. And then she looked at him over her shoulder, joy tinged with a hint of hesitation. "This is for me?"

He came up to join her. It had taken him several hours to hunt this up. "This used to be mine," he told her. "But it's a little too small for me now and it's been rather sad, sitting all alone in storage. So I'd take it as a personal favor if you used it."

Excited, the girl shifted from foot to foot as if about to break into an impromptu game of hopscotch. "Where's your new one?"

He laughed, shaking his head. "I don't have one."

"You don't paint anymore?" Surprise was imprinted on every inch of the small heart-shaped face.

It was a long story, built on rebellion and not one to tell a child, even a child as stunningly intelligent as Kelli. The easel had never really been put to use and he was surprised he'd saved it. But to keep things simple, he merely said, "No."

Surprise was replaced with sympathy. It was obvious Kelli felt that everyone should experience the joy of painting. Reclaiming her hand from her mother, she patted his. "Bet you could ask your mom to get you one and to give you lessons," she told him.

It was an effort to retain a straight face. She was darling as well as intelligent and gifted. "She's a very busy lady."

Kelli nodded slowly, absorbing the excuse and its ramifications. And then suddenly, her head bobbed up, her eyes shining as she looked at him. "I could teach you." Saying it out loud reinforced her enthusiasm and she clapped her hands together. "I could. It'd be fun."

He thought of all the years in his past that he'd actively turned down every attempt his mother made to mate him with a paintbrush and a canvas. He had staunchly refused to enter her world, wanting one of his own to colonize and leave his mark on.

But with this small, eager little face looking up at him, all that melted away. "Maybe it would be," he allowed. "I'll see if I can find another easel for tomorrow."

Kelli's smile grew even wider. "Good."

God, she sounded more adult that half the people he knew, Philippe thought, completely charmed. He noted that J.D. had placed all of her daughter's jars of paint along the easel's edge and mounted the painting against it.

"Call if you need me," she instructed Kelli, then stepped away from the child. The slanted glance that came his way indicated that she wanted him to follow. When he did, she asked, "How much do I owe you?"

He'd followed her literally, but now she'd lost him. "For what?"

Her voice low, she was all but whispering. "The easel."

What kind of a person did she think he was, pretending to give a child a gift only to have her mother pay for it under the table? Maybe she was used to strings being attached to things. So he set her straight. "What I told your daughter was true. That used to be my easel. There is no charge," he informed her firmly.

She wasn't comfortable about this, didn't want him getting the wrong idea even though instinctively, part of her did like him for the gesture. Maybe that was the part that scared her. More than a little. "I know, but—"

"Just consider it a gift from me to Kelli." His eyes met hers. He saw the wariness. "No strings attached."

She took a breath, wondering if she was making a mistake, believing him. She had to work at keeping their relationship strictly professional.

Good luck with that, a voice in her head mocked. She'd

already brought him food yesterday and brought her daughter along to work today. *Not exactly proceeding according to strict professional guidelines here, are we, J.D?*

She forced a smile to her lips, trying to quell the nervous feeling in her stomach. "That was a very nice thing you did."

"I like seeing her smile," Philippe told her honestly. He watched her mouth curve and could have sworn something tightened inside of him. "You have the same smile," he observed.

Urges began to form, swarming over him out of nowhere. Or maybe, out of a somewhere he had no business visiting. Because something told him that J. D. Wyatt wasn't just a casual date. J.D. was the kind of woman you made plans with. Solid plans. And there was nothing in his world to suggest he had a solid plan. Look at the examples he had to follow, the parents he'd had. The norm when he was growing up was here today, gone tomorrow.

He shoved his hands into his back pockets, curbing the very strong desire to touch her face, to trace his fingers along the curve of her mouth and commit it to memory.

Damn, where was this coming from?

He cleared his throat. "I guess I'd better get back to work."

"Yeah." The words tasted like powdered spackle. "Me, too," she murmured.

Gordon reentered the room, bringing along his own

set of long neglected tools. He glanced from his sister to Philippe, then watched as the latter left the room. Setting the toolbox down, Gordon crossed over to his sister. "Something going on between you two?" he asked mildly, in the same tone he might have used if he was asking about that day's temperature projection.

The question startled Janice, throwing cold water on what might have been a moment's worth of revelry. Groundless revelry, she insisted. Trust Gordon to be blunt.

"No." She went into the kitchen. "What makes you think that?"

He laughed dryly. "Looked like a lot of chemistry and heat flashing back and forth from where I was standing."

She looked down at his shoes. "Must be some loose wiring running under your feet," she decided innocently. "Maybe you'd better examine it later just to be safe. Wouldn't want this place going up, especially after all the work we're going to put into it."

"Guy doesn't give a woman's little girl an easel because there's loose wiring in the floor," he observed.

Janice sighed, refusing to entertain the thought of what Gordon was suggesting. Philippe was her client. If he liked the job she did for him, she had no doubt he would refer other people to her. There was nothing more to their relationship. Besides, she was not about to get involved with anyone. She'd never been able to get through to her father, never had that magical moment she'd waited for where he saw how much she loved him, how much she wanted him to be proud of her. And as for her husband, well that had never had a chance to go anywhere, so she would never know. She had been a wife and a widow within six months. That had had its own set of pain attached. She didn't need to seek out more.

Besides, she had enough to keep her busy. She had Kelli and her work. There wasn't space for more than that, certainly not for another pass at having her heart broken.

"Make yourself useful, Gordon."

He grinned at her. "I thought I already was, since you can't seem to see the forest for the trees—" He scratched his head. "Or is it the trees for the forest? I always get that confused."

That wasn't the only thing he got confused, she thought. "It's the floor for the debris," she declared, pointing to the very large pile of splintered wood veneer and plasterboard, the end results of her swinging her sledgehammer at the kitchen cabinets yesterday. Philippe had sent her home before she'd had a chance to remove the debris. "Clean it up."

He could have taken exception to her tone. Once, when his father's company had been his, he'd been her boss. And even when they'd worked with their father, he had supposedly always been the one in charge. It was only after the company went bankrupt and Janice began getting jobs on her own and throwing some of the business his way that she started issuing orders.

Gordon saluted her, his expression suddenly somber. "I'm on it."

"Good to know," she murmured. She didn't want to repay Philippe's kindness by appearing to take advantage of him.

Stooping down, she filled her arms with splintered plasterboard and got started.

He wasn't in his office.

Janice glanced at her watch to check the time. It was close to eleven and she'd assumed that he'd be busy at his work. She'd deliberately gone out of her way to pass his office to talk to him.

Can't talk to an empty chair.

Had he gone out and she'd missed hearing him leave? She'd begun work on gutting the downstairs powder room and wanted to have all her ducks in a row. Or at least swimming in the right direction.

She'd brought a color chart so that Philippe could decide what color he wanted her to paint the walls.

Shrugging, she tucked the chart under her arm and went back out again. It was getting close to lunchtime anyway. She might as well collect Kelli and her brother and get something to eat. Because this was their first day on a job together, she thought she'd take them both out to celebrate the occasion instead of just bringing lunch from home.

Janice moved around the corner. She didn't have to

look to know that Kelli would be completely captivated with her work. Painting always summoned this font of joy from within her, even when it wasn't going well. With her sunny disposition, Kelli always managed to see the bright side of everything.

"Kelli, honey," she called out, "we're going to break for lunch. Would you like to be the one to pick the restaurant?"

It always made her daughter feel so grown up when she could choose where they would all go to eat. And then she laughed to herself. Before she knew it, Kelli *would* be an adult. God knew the little girl was growing up much too fast, doing ten years for every candle she blew out.

When she received no response, Janice quickened her pace and made her way through the dining room toward the alcove. The moment she came near the threshold, she could feel her heart thudding in her chest.

Could, unaccountably, feel a sting in her eyes.

Allergies, she told herself.

Philippe was standing behind Kelli, guiding her hand, giving her instructions in a low, patient voice. It was a father-daughter scene worthy of a holiday card.

Except that they weren't a father and daughter.

So what? she demanded silently. Her own father had never been that patient on the rare occasions he explained something to her. Most of the time, he'd waved her back with that trite, archaic sentiment that "girls don't need to know that." She'd learned her trade by watching, by sneaking behind her father's back to observe him in action.

Never once had he put a hammer or a screwdriver into her hand and shown her how to use it. No tips or secrets were passed to her the way they had been to Gordon. Except that Gordon wanted no part of it. He remained, pretending to listen, because he was afraid not to. But his mind was always preoccupied with the current flavor of the month he was squiring. He'd been there in body, but not in spirit.

She would have killed for a moment like this in her own life. And Kelli was obviously lapping it all up, she thought, watching the way her daughter beamed up at Philippe.

Greeting-card moment or not, she had to break this up. "Kel, we're going out to lunch."

But Kelli was completely focused on the images she was creating on the canvas and the technique Philippe was showing her. "In a minute, Mama."

She knew better than to let herself be ignored. "Now, honey."

Philippe removed his hand from Kelli's and stepped back. "You'd better listen to your mother, Kelli."

The resigned sigh was filled with disappointment. Kelli retired her brush. "Okay." And then she looked at her mother hopefully. "Can Philippe come, too?"

She had to nip this in the bud, too. "His name is Mr. Zabelle, Kelli," she reminded her daughter. "And I'm sure Mr. Zabelle has better things to do than come to eat with us."

He was about to take the excuse she tendered. He'd

already spent way too much time not doing his work. So no one was more surprised than he was to hear himself say, "Actually, I don't." He was looking at J.D. rather than the little girl. "Unless of course, you'd rather I didn't come along."

Her mouth felt like she'd been snacking on sandpaper since morning. Janice knew she should be blunt and say something about lunch being a family affair. The truth was she didn't want him around her because he made her uncomfortable—but he only made her uncomfortable because she wanted to be around him. It was a conundrum, as her father had been fond of saying.

The simplest way to avoid all that, to avoid any explanations that would probably result in her turning redder than the color of the shoes that Kelli had insisted on wearing this morning, was to say, "No, by all means, the more the merrier. Of course you can join us for lunch."

So, she did.

Chapter Ten

As it turned out, Philippe seemed to hit it off very well with Gordon and if one or the other paused to take a breath, there was Kelli, chatting like a little old lady, eager to fill in the dead air.

Consequently, Janice contributed very little to the conversation that took place over salads and seasoned chicken strips. Her exact words were: "Thank you," uttered twice and neither time to the people sitting around her at the table. The words were addressed to the waitress who brought her beverage and then her lunch.

Content to observe and listen, both with a measure of awe, Janice assumed that no one noticed her silence.

It amazed her that not only Kelli but Gordon seemed to be completely taken with Philippe. Their reasons, however, were obviously different. Kelli hung on the man's every word because she was apparently caught up in a spate of hero-worship. As for Gordon, even though he and Philippe appeared to be worlds apart, the two had some things in common.

Would wonders never cease?

So as Gordon and Philippe talked about sports and action movies, and Kelli interjected enthusiastically from time to time, Janice took in the exchange and smiled to herself. And tried not to notice the feeling of contentment that wrapped itself around her.

"You didn't talk much at lunch."

Janice sucked in her breath, startled. Preoccupied with gathering her things together, she hadn't heard Philippe come up behind her. Hadn't seen him at all for the last four hours, not since they're returned and she had gotten back to work.

Turning, she looked up into brilliant green eyes that took her breath away.

"You, Gordon and Kelli didn't leave any openings to get a word in edgewise." Her pulse was dancing, she noted. He was standing too close. "I'm surprised you even noticed."

His mouth curved just the slightest bit. "Hard not to notice things about you."

It wasn't a line. He looked incapable of grinding out lines, she decided. Which made him completely different from her brother, Gordon, and probably his brother, Georges, too, she'd wager. From his manner, and the fact that he'd winked at her as she left, she had strong suspicions that Georges was much like her own brother.

She could feel Philippe's eyes working their way along her face, studying her. Looking right *into* her.

Heat traveled up her body as a blush worked its way to the roots of her hair.

Now that had to be a sight, she thought disparagingly. A twenty-eight-year-old woman, widowed and a single mother to boot, who had, if not been around the block a few times, at least had gotten off the family stoop, blushing.

She caught herself wishing that the house didn't catch too much of the afternoon sun. There was no way the man could miss the fact that she was blushing like some adolescent school girl.

"Thank you," she murmured, acknowledging his compliment. "For everything."

"Everything?"

She elaborated. "The easel, lunch." *Hiring me in the first place.* She caught her lower lip between her teeth, debating her next words, but she didn't want him getting the wrong idea.

"You know I didn't invite you along with us to pay for it."

A surge of desire rose out of nowhere, making him want to nibble on the same lip she'd carelessly taken prisoner. Did she have any idea how delectable she was?

"As I recall, you didn't invite me at all," he contradicted. "That was Kelli's doing."

He was right. Janice shrugged. "I thought you'd be uncomfortable."

Although he wasn't as outgoing as either one of his brothers, because of the kind of life he'd led with his mother during his childhood, he was able to fit into almost any situation.

"I wasn't uncomfortable." His eyes searched her face. "Were you?"

She had been, but it wasn't the kind of uncomfortable he meant. It was the "uncomfortable" of realizing that feelings were being roused, feelings that could only lead to disappointment. But her thoughts were her own, not to be shared with someone who was, for all intents and purposes, a stranger.

She lifted her chin defiantly. "Why should I be uncomfortable?"

"I don't know." He watched her, the soul of innocence. Innocence about to go awry. "I'm harmless enough."

Had the man even *looked* in the mirror recently? She laughed shortly. "Not hardly."

He could listen to the sound of her laughter all day, even when it was aimed at him. "Care to elaborate?"

She shook her head. Tiny pinpricks of panic assaulted

her body. That was the trouble when you brought your brother and daughter with you, she thought. You couldn't just beat a hasty retreat and drive away. You had to collect them first. "No."

It was an effort to keep his hands at his sides. A stray hair along her cheek begged to be pushed back into place. "Then I was right, I do make you uncomfortable."

He made her fidget inside. Made her restless.

Made her remember that there were other things besides two by fours to put her hand to. Small, nameless desires materialized out of the mists where they'd been banished. She yearned to touch this man, to feel his muscles beneath her fingertips, his stubble against her cheek in the morning. Yearned to catch a whiff of his scent on the pillow beside hers even after he was gone.

God, but she missed being part of a twosome. She and Gary had had their problems, but it wasn't anything that couldn't have been worked out in time. She'd married him to get out of her father's house, where she felt unloved and ignored. All she'd wanted was to begin a life of her own, to matter to someone. That was her goal and she was willing to make all kinds of compromises to reach it.

But then Gary had gone and died on her. Leaving her just as her mother had. Just as her father had, in his own way, years before he died. With her parents, she'd endured emotional abandonment before they ever left her physically. With Gary, it had been physical, but this didn't lessen the pain of the loss.

There were just so many times she could expose her heart. She no longer needed approval, she was her own person. And as for love, well, Kelli loved her and in his own confused way, so did Gordon. That was enough.

Oh God, he was touching her, his fingertips moving against her face. It took everything she had not to melt into Philippe's hand, not to melt against him. Her breath backed up in her lungs.

"I don't mean to make you uncomfortable, J.D."

"Janice," she whispered.

He leaned in a little closer, his lips so close to hers, she could almost feel them moving as he asked, "What?"

It was an effort to think, to speak. "You've hired me, that means you get the right to call me by my first name."

"Janice." He nodded, repeating the name. And then he smiled. "It suits you."

"How so?" Damn it, was he ever going to drop his hand? She was having trouble thinking.

He didn't know how much longer he could refrain from acting on the impulse that kept doubling in size every second. "Short, to the point, yet feminine."

That made her laugh under her breath and she shook her head. "Been a long time since anyone called me feminine."

Very slowly, he moved his thumb along her lower lip, enticing them both. "Don't see why. You are. Under those jeans and that T-shirt, you are."

What the hell was he doing? his conscience demanded. It was like having some kind of out-of-body experience. He'd somehow stepped outside of himself and now he watched this unfold. Watched himself flirt with a woman even though any relationship would be doomed from the start. He knew he wasn't going to follow up on any of these feelings he was having, even if they were so strong they made it hard for him to breathe.

He was his mother's son, which meant that no matter what he felt now, he was going to move on. Something always seemed to stop him, made him turn away, before he became even mildly serious. Janice didn't deserve to have her life messed up like that.

He needed to stop, to walk away.

Now.

But he didn't. And he was no longer just watching, he was acting. Acting on impulse, on whim, on a desire that seemed to be bigger than he was, acting like some kind of fool.

It didn't change anything. He leaned over her trim, athletic body and brought his mouth down on hers.

Anticipation did not overshadow reality. If anything, it was the other way around. For a moment, he allowed himself to forget everything, just enjoy the moment.

Oh, my God. Everything around her, the room, the house, the world, everything faded to black and disappeared except for the incredible sensations shooting through her. Absorbing her. Breaking down from the mini-tower of strength she perceived herself to be and re-building a flesh and blood woman with needs and desires.

Without thinking, she rose up on her toes as far as she could, winding her arms around his neck and leaning into him, nerves jumping all up and down on her body. She'd never expected anything like this, never had her head turned completely around by a mere kiss.

No, not mere. Anything but mere.

"Mere" didn't make her skin sizzle or her brain go careening. But as wondrous as it was, she felt unsettled. Unsettled because his kiss opened up floodgates she was terrified of having unlocked.

And yet—

This was delicious and she didn't want it to stop. In a minute, but not now. Just a second longer and then she'd back away. She had to. No matter what her yearning was, she couldn't act on it. Because she wasn't alone.

Thank God she'd brought her brother and Kelli with her. Having them here forced her to remain on the straight and narrow path, something she strongly doubted she could have done on her own right now.

And then, as unexpectedly as it had begun, it was over.

Philippe drew his head back, his expression dazed. He took a breath, as if to steady himself. It was going to take more than a breath to do that for her, she thought.

"I'm not going to apologize," he told her.

"All right." She was fairly surprised she could

actually talk. Her lips felt as if they had the consistency of warmed honey.

"Not for the kiss, anyway."

She didn't understand, but then, it would have taken her a minute to respond if someone had asked her her name. "Then for what?"

The smile was sad and burrowed into her heart before she could stop it. "For more things than I can begin to tell you."

"You are a very complicated, mysterious man, Philippe Zabelle."

The laugh was dry with only a touch of humor to it. "You don't know the half of it."

He made her wonder. About the sadness in his eyes, about him. Had there been anyone in his life? Someone who'd hurt him? Or someone he'd hurt that he felt guilty about?

"Maybe someday I will," she replied.

Damn it, not your business, Janice. This wasn't part of the job and that was all she needed to focus on. Abruptly, she raised her voice and called out to her daughter.

"Time to call it a day, kiddo." *While Mama still had knees that functioned.*

She felt as if she'd just been dynamited off her comfortable perch. With effort she slowed her pace and left the room, trying very hard not to look as if she was hurrying away from him.

But she was.

* * *

As she carried in the laundry basket from the garage later that evening, she noticed that Gordon's car wasn't there. Still holding the basket, she passed by the window and glanced out.

The car wasn't parked at the curb, either. "Kelli, where's Uncle Gordon?"

The little girl looked up from the book of children's drawings she was paging through. "He went out."

Oh God, not on a date, Janice prayed. The only time Gordon didn't say anything about leaving, didn't call out a "see you later," he was going off on a date with someone he knew he shouldn't be seeing.

Janice set down the basket on the coffee table and sat down beside her daughter on the sofa. "Out? When?"

"A little while ago." Kelli paused to think. "The seven o'clock news lady was on. He said I couldn't go with him."

The idea of Kelli out with Gordon on one of his dates horrified her. "Well, at least he has some grain of sense," she murmured to herself, then looked at her daughter. Something wasn't adding up. "Why would you want to go with him?"

"Because he's going to Phili— Mr. Zabelle's house," Kelli amended, knowing that her mother didn't like her calling grown-ups by their first names.

Janice stared at her daughter. Okay, the two men seemed to get along at lunch, but Gordon just wasn't in

Philippe's league. Philippe had things together while Gordon was a loosely wound ball of yarn, ready to come apart at the slightest push. "Why would he be going there?"

"To play poker," Kelli volunteered brightly.

Janice's mouth dropped open. Poker? Had he gotten caught up in a new obsession? Gordon didn't do things by half measures. If he started seeing someone, he was planning marriage by the end of the first date. She'd seen him through a number of dependencies, including food and alcohol. He didn't know how to do anything in moderation—except work, she thought cynically. These days, she was working like a dog not only to pay her own bills, but to help Gordon meet his bankruptcy payments as well. The faster that was paid off, the sooner he'd be able to get on his own two feet.

A cold shiver went down her spine. That wasn't going to happen if he'd taken up gambling.

She rose to her feet, putting her hand out to her daughter. "C'mon, honey."

Kelli scooted off the sofa, taking her mother's hand. "Where are we going?"

"Well, you're going to Mrs. Addison." A grandmother three times over, the woman had made it known that she was willing to babysit in the evenings, especially if there was an emergency. This definitely qualified. "I'm going to Mr. Zabelle's house to bring back Uncle Gordon before he finds another pit to fall into."

It was obvious that Kelli didn't quite understand what

she was talking about, but she'd latched onto the one thing that was clear to her. Her mother was going to see Philippe. "Mr. Zabelle? Why can't I go with you?"

Janice grabbed her purse out of the closet. Slinging it over her shoulder, she headed for the front door with Kelli in tow. "Because Mama's going to be using some grown-up words that you're too young to hear."

"I watch TV, Mama," Kelli protested.

She locked the door behind her. "More grown-up than that," Janice told her tersely.

Her tone was far from warm, but it wasn't meant for Kelli. She was focused on Gordon, annoyed with him for blundering into yet another possible addiction. She wasn't overly thrilled with Philippe either, even though the man had no way of knowing about her brother's addictive personality.

But he would by the time the evening was through.

This was all she needed, Janice thought.

She struggled to keep her temper in-check. As she drove to Philippe's, it was an effort to keep from pressing down on the accelerator and going over the speed limit.

For most of her adult life, she'd been bailing her brother out of one thing or another. His inability to recognize that he was being taken in by a series of women who only wanted what he could give them, had catapulted him into bankruptcy, which had led him into drinking and then overeating. She'd finally, finally gotten him to come around and be her assistant on these contracting jobs. And now he was sliding backward into something new.

She pressed her lips together, trying not to swear as she eased her foot off the gas. She was doing five miles over the speed limit.

Philippe was a bright man, couldn't he see that Gordon had a weak, malleable personality?

Damn it, why did she have to be her brother's keeper, anyway? She had enough to keep her busy.

Getting over that kiss, for instance.

The second she thought of it, of her involuntary reaction, Janice felt her skin tingling.

Get a grip, Janice. You're supposed to be boiling mad, not a bowl of mush.

By the time she arrived at Philippe's door, Janice was completely worked up. Instead of ringing the bell, she knocked. Pounded was more like it. The door had taken the place of her brother's head.

Inside, Alain peered at his brother over a hand that would have gladdened the heart of a professional gambler.

Slim fingers folded the cards in his hand. Alain raised a quizzical eyebrow. "You expecting someone to come break down your door, Philippe?"

"Not tonight." The pounding continued. He sighed, folded his cards and placed them facedown on the table.

As he rose, he pointed to the hand. "Don't anyone try to mess with that, I know what I have."

"An unhealthy distrust of your relatives is what you have," Georges commented. "Philippe's blunt warning wasn't meant for you," he told Gordon. "He thinks we cheat. In reality, he's not that hot a poker player."

Gordon nodded, finding himself completely at ease in this company of men. It was a pleasant feeling, one he wasn't accustomed to.

Philippe waved a hand at Georges. "I don't cheat," he declared as he opened the door. Turning, he was surprised and not a little pleased to see Janice standing there.

Her eyes were blazing. And there was something very stirring about the image she presented. "Did I forget something?"

"Yes," she snapped, not waiting to be invited in. "Decency."

He closed the door behind her. "No, I'm pretty sure I stocked up on that the last time I was at the store." She wasn't smiling. "What's the matter?"

By now, she was no longer thinking rationally. God only knew how much Gordon could have lost. "How could you?" she demanded.

Philippe hadn't a clue. "How could I what?"

She gritted her teeth. Without her experience of plucking Gordon out of precarious situations, she might have thought Philippe was innocent. "How could you invite my brother to your poker game?"

Philippe shoved his hands into his front pockets. Eventually this was going to make sense. He just had to be patient. "Pretty easily, actually. I said something like, 'Gordon, want to come to a game I'm holding tonight?' And he said yes."

She struggled to keep her voice down. She didn't want to embarrass her brother in front of other people, but she certainly didn't want to have to bail him out any more than she was already doing.

"This isn't funny, Zabelle," she told him in a low, firm voice. "Gordon's got an addictive personality. He doesn't do anything in half measures." She was rambling, she thought and reined herself in. "I can't go into details, but this is really a very bad thing. You have to cut him off."

Philippe still looked like the soul of innocence as he asked her, "You want me to cut off his colored toothpicks?"

About to shout "yes" she stopped and stared at him. "Colored toothpicks?"

He nodded, taking her arm. Thinking he was going to usher her out, she pulled it away. "That's what we play for. Colored toothpicks."

She wasn't about to be distracted. There had to be more than that. "But they represent something, don't they?"

Philippe nodded. "Well, yeah."

To his credit, Zabelle didn't even try to lie about it.

Although that didn't change the bottom line. "Gordon can't afford it."

Very complacently, Philippe placed his hands on her shoulders. That he was so calm only infuriated her further. "Janice, calm down. If he's the big loser, he has to wash the big winner's car or clean the big winner's barbecue grill. Something along those lines."

The fire went out of her eyes. "What? You don't gamble for money?"

He shook his head. "We play for things, chores mostly. Playing relaxes us and it gives us a chance to get together." He took a breath. Maybe she'd feel better if he explained a few things to her. Ordinarily, he didn't like getting personal, but he made an exception. "My father was a professional gambler and he 'professionally' lost almost everything my mother worked for. I don't even play the slot machines in Vegas. I don't believe in real gambling, but this is just harmless fun, a way to knock off steam, get the adrenaline to kick in without any risk."

She caught her lower lip between her teeth, feeling somewhat foolish now. "Really?"

He laced his hand through hers. "Really." He nodded toward the dining room. "Come see."

"No, that's okay," she demurred. But he was already bringing her in.

Like a boy caught by his mother after curfew, Gordon looked both surprised and uneasy to see her. "What are you doing here?"

Before she could say anything, Philippe was quick to explain. "Janice thought she forgot one of her tools. I wanted to introduce her to you guys—in case any of you lugs has a remodeling job you want done." Turning to her, he confided, "All of them are as handy as dried out paste."

Georges merely laughed. "You should talk. At least I know what to do with pointy objects."

Just standing there, listening to the exchange, she could feel the love in the room. It made her envious and long for a childhood she'd never had.

Chapter Eleven

As Philippe introduced her to the other members of his weekly poker game, Janice was acutely aware of the way her brother was looking at her. As if he knew why she was really there. It wasn't because of some so-called imaginary tool she'd left behind. She wanted to check up on him, as if he were twelve and she was his mother.

It was all there in his face: annoyance at her unexpected invasion, hurt at her lack of trust. But damn it, could he really blame her? After all he'd put her through? She only had his best interests at heart.

The introductions over, Janice pressed her lips

together and mustered a smile that took in all the men gathered around the oblong table.

"Sorry, I didn't know I'd be barging in on a poker game. Please, go back to playing." Her eyes met Gordon's briefly. "I was never here." She glanced at Philippe. He made a move to follow her as she backed away from the table. "I can see myself out." Again, her eyes shifted toward her brother. "See you at home, Gordon," she added as she retreated.

Despite what she'd just told him, Philippe followed her out of the room.

She felt just awful for raising her voice and accusing Philippe of taking advantage of her brother. She wouldn't blame him if he decided to terminate their contract. But before she could tender an apology, something that never came easily to her, Philippe took her by the arm and drew her over to the side.

"Listen," he began softly, "I'm sorry I stirred things up for you."

God, when he looked at her like that with those green eyes of his, she caught herself thinking that she could forgive him for just about anything.

Get a grip, Janice. He's the guy you're working for right now, nothing else. Is that clear?

Clear as mud.

"It seemed harmless enough at the time," Philippe was saying to her. She struggled to focus on his words and not his lips or his eyes. Not exactly easy, given their proximity. "I got the feeling earlier today that your brother's struggling with a lot of problems and I thought this might help him blow off steam. It does me."

What kind of problems did Philippe have, she wondered. From everything she'd seen, he led a perfect life.

After a beat, she found her tongue and discovered that it really wasn't glued to the roof of her mouth. "You don't have to apologize to me."

The grin was quick, so was the all-but-lethal shot to her gut. "Well, apparently I do. I don't know if you realized it or not, but there was steam coming out of your ears when you got here and I think you left a perfect replica of your knuckles on my door."

Okay, so she'd overreacted. Big time. She wasn't the kind to try to bury a mistake. When she was wrong, she was wrong and she admitted it, but she wanted Philippe to understand why she'd come in looking and sounding like a possessed wild woman.

She just wasn't sure how to begin. Or how much to tell him. "Gordon's done some pretty stupid things in his time."

To his credit, Philippe didn't prod her for details. "It's a big club."

Because he didn't ask, she was more inclined to share a little more. Gordon liked to talk and she had no doubts that her brother would wind up telling Philippe the whole story sooner than later, so she wasn't violating any kind of trust by letting the man know now.

"No, I mean *really* stupid. He lets himself be led around by the nose by any woman who'll pay attention to him." She shrugged helplessly. "Could be an offshoot of our mother walking out on us. He was very attached to her."

Janice stopped abruptly, having gone further than she'd intended. The last sentence had just slipped out without warning.

Philippe nodded slowly, as if analyzing what she'd just said. "And it hit him hard when the reverse didn't turn out to be true." He stood there for a long moment, studying her. She caught herself wanting to shift beneath his gaze. It took effort to remain still. "How about you?"

Unconsciously, she raised her chin. "How about me, what?"

"How did your mother's walking out on the family affect you?"

Janice looked away and shrugged, as if it hadn't bothered her. As if she hadn't stayed up nights when she was a little girl, wondering if there was something she could have done better to make her mother stay. Guilt had been her constant companion for the first two years after the family had gone from four to three members.

"I didn't think about it one way or another," she lied. Because it felt as if his eyes were peering straight into her soul, she added, "I guess she wanted to be away from my father more than she wanted to be with us."

"We have something in common," he told her. When Janice eyed him quizzically, he said, "We both had gypsy mothers."

She'd read somewhere about Lily Moreau's bohemian lifestyle. She supposed he was trying to make her feel better about the situation. Too late, she thought, she no longer felt anything about it one way or another. "Yes, but with one difference. Yours came back."

"And left. And came back. And then left again." He laughed softly, having come to terms with it years ago. "Made for a very confused childhood. There were lots of times when we saw the nanny and the housekeeper more than we saw our mother."

If there were any problems, they must have been minor, she thought. Georges was charming and Alain seemed to be as well. And as for Philippe, well Philippe was as together and well-adjusted a person as she'd ever come across. Just a little withdrawn. But that seemed to be changing.

"You and your brothers seemed to have turned out all right."

"So did you," he pointed out. "We all do what we have to do to survive." Now that he looked at her closely, she seemed incredibly tense, like someone waiting not for the next shoe to fall but the next bomb to go off. He tried to make her feel more at ease, more hopeful. "I get the impression that Gordon's trying to come around."

She closed her eyes for a moment. *If only.* "I hope

so. I can't keep bailing him out." Philippe was smiling like he knew something she didn't.

"Sure you can," he told her. Though she might protest otherwise, he had a feeling that she was one of those people for whom family loyalty meant everything. He could readily identify with that. "You wouldn't be you if you didn't."

"You don't know so much about me."

Philippe laughed. Now there she was very, very wrong. "Sorry to contradict you, but this is the age of the Internet, Janice. I know a great deal about you."

God help her, she liked the way he said her name, as if it was purely feminine. As if *she* was purely feminine. When had she last felt that way? Other than when he kissed her, she amended.

"I know that you worked for your father at his construction company," he told her. "That he left Wyatt Construction to Gordon, not you. That within a very short period of time Gordon had to file a chapter 13 because he had borrowed so heavily against the company's assets that Wyatt Construction couldn't afford to pay its men. And then the company wound up paying penalties because it couldn't finish jobs in accordance with the deadlines in the contracts.

"I know that you have a contractor's license." She'd told him that, but he stunned her by reciting the number, something she *hadn't* told him. "And you're presently trying to regain your footing so that you can finally form your own company—after you finish paying off your brother's bills."

For a moment, there was nothing but silence in the hallway. How could there be that much information floating around about her? But then, in this paperless society, everything seemed to be drifting out there in cyberspace, waiting to be netted and pulled in like a school of salmon. Still, she couldn't get over how extensive a job he'd done.

"You looked me up?"

He nodded. "Can't just let anyone take a sledgehammer to my house," he told her. He'd investigated her after he'd hired her. Motivated, he had to admit, more by curiosity about the woman than a desire to protect himself against the possible rash actions of a stranger.

Philippe shoved his hands into his pockets, knowing she probably wouldn't like the next suggestion. But sometimes, being there for a person meant *not* being there for them 24-7. It came under the prickly heading of tough love. "Maybe Gordon should start paying off his own bills. It would probably make him feel better about himself."

Funny, ordinarily she'd resent someone giving her advice on how to handle her brother. But there was something in Philippe's eyes that told her he meant well. Besides, he was a brother, too. As the oldest, he probably knew what it meant to be there for one or both of them.

Janice shook her head. "The only money Gordon seems to make these days is the money I pay him when

I have a job that's too big for just me. Whether I hand him the money so he can pay the bills or I just pay the bills myself, it all boils down to my paying the monthly bills. Pretending it's anything else is just an illusion."

She watched, mesmerized, as his mouth curved again. Making her pulse skip. "We all need illusions to sustain us."

She sighed, knowing she didn't have all the answers. Lately, it felt as if she had very few of them. "Maybe you're right."

"I am." The quick grin went directly to his eyes. And to her central core. Janice had to concentrate not to let her breath back up. Not to allow her imagination to run away with her. "At least fifty percent of the time."

"Hey, big spender," Alain called from the dining room, "your hand's getting cold. You gonna come back and play or not?"

"You'd better go." Janice nodded toward the rear of the house, feeling guilty about having monopolized him. "Your hand is calling."

Maybe it was, but other things called to him as well, he thought. Things that had nothing to do with a hand of poker. Standing here at the threshold of his home, the lighting sparse, he was incredibly aware of almost everything about her. Aware of her close proximity, of the way her chest rose and fell with each breath.

Damn, but he had this overwhelming urge to kiss her again.

He would have acted on it, but he knew that one of his brothers, cousins or even her brother could come out looking for him. The last thing he wanted was to embarrass her. So he tightened his resolve and remained where he was, on the tip of the fence and dying to fall over to her side.

"Yeah," he murmured. "Maybe I'd better go. See you tomorrow."

She nodded, turning to go. And then she turned around again. "Oh." The single word had him pivoting on his heel, looking at her again. "I meant to tell you, about my bringing Kelli today, it's not going to be a permanent thing. I really am trying to find a babysitter for her during the day."

Philippe shook his head. "Don't."

"Don't what?"

"Don't get another babysitter for her. I think it might upset her to be left behind with someone new. Besides, it's important for a child to be around her mother." He remembered how he'd felt every time he'd seen his mother go out the door, wondering if it was for the afternoon or if he wouldn't be seeing her for weeks at a clip. Lily never liked telling him and his brothers that she was taking off. She left that up to the nanny or her husband-of-the-moment.

Years later, in an off moment, she'd confided that the disappointed expression on his face stayed with her for days, marring her joy over an upcoming show. It was easier for her just to slip away, like a mother leaving her child on the first day of kindergarten.

He'd caught on about her getaways long before she'd made her confession. Caught on and rather than confront her the next time she returned, worked at living his life without any parental support or input. He told himself it didn't matter that she took off without warning as frequently as she did.

But in his heart, in the place where secrets were locked up, he knew that it did. And that, too, made him leery of attachments. Because attachments meant disappointments.

"All right," she said slowly. She knew that Kelli would be more than happy to come along with her to work. She was relieved that she wouldn't have to face telling her daughter that she was getting a new baby-sitter, someone besides Mrs. McClonsky or Gordon. And she *really* hadn't been looking forward to the tedious round of interviews for someone suitable to watch her daughter. Her eyes smiled at him, telegraphing her relief.

"If you're sure you don't mind."

"I'm sure I don't mind," he assured her. "She's a good kid, not to mention gifted."

Janice wondered if he really believed that or if he was just saying it because every mother liked hearing such things.

Stop overanalyzing everything, she upbraided

herself. *Sometimes a raindrop is just a raindrop and not the beginning of a flash flood.*

Heartened, she drew back her shoulders and nodded amiably. "Okay, see you tomorrow."

"Hey, Philippe—" Beau called, his voice all but booming.

"Coming. Keep your shirt on." Philippe looked at her, suppressing, again, the urge to kiss her. "I'll send him back early," he promised.

And then winked.

Obviously, winking was a family thing, Janice thought as she left. Except that when Georges had winked at her, her stomach hadn't suddenly flipped over and tied itself up in a knot.

She tried not to think about that as she all but flew back to her truck.

The front door squeaked as it opened then closed. Gordon cursed under his breath, thinking for the dozenth time that he needed to oil that. The squeak prevented him from making an otherwise silent entrance home.

The second he heard the noise, he saw Janice. His sister had been stretched out on the sofa, a book housed on her chest, her eyes closed. They flew open as the squeak penetrated her consciousness. She'd always been an incredibly light sleeper. Unlike their father. But then, she didn't have a quart of wine to lull her to sleep each night the way their father had.

He might as well face the music, he thought, walking into the living room. "Look, maybe I shouldn't have snuck out of the house that way," Gordon began awkwardly, feeling like some tongue-tied teenager instead of a man talking to his sister. His *younger* sister, for Pete's sakes.

Still a little bleary-eyed, Janice stifled a yawn and sat up. It took her a second to pull herself together. She wasn't waiting up to take him to task, she was waiting up to apologize.

"I'm sorry I made you feel that you had to sneak out." Her words, she saw, surprised him. "It's just that I worry about you."

It wasn't that he didn't like her caring about him, it was just that sometimes it made him feel like he was in a straitjacket.

"Yeah, I know." He shrugged. "But I think I'm good, now. Really." He perched for a second on the arm of the sofa, right beside her. "I mean, I learned my lesson. Hell, bankruptcy, losing Pop's company. Even if I didn't like the company, I didn't mean for any of those things to happen," he told her, silently asking her forgiveness for having screwed up so badly.

"I know." Shifting over, she put her arm on his shoulder, reaching up as far as she could. "I know." She rose to her feet, tossing the book down on the coffee table. The bookmark slipped out. She picked it up and left it on top of the book, too tired to search for the passage it had been marking. "Well, I'm going to bed."

He stared at her back, dumbfounded as she began to walk away. "Don't you want to know how I did?"

Since it wasn't for money, fear had been taken out of the equation. "Okay, how d'you do?"

"I won." He was grinning like a kid who'd been awarded a lifetime supply of his favorite flavor of ice cream. "Philippe's brother, Alain, has to wash my car. Did you know he's studying to be a lawyer?" That part pleased him the most, having an almost-lawyer working for him, however briefly.

"No," she admitted, "I didn't know that." She didn't know very much about Philippe and his family. Nowhere near the amount of information that Philippe had amassed on her, she thought. Maybe it was time she put her hand to the Internet—tomorrow, she added silently, stifling another yawn.

"Maybe I should have gone to law school," he murmured under his breath, following her up the stairs to his own bedroom.

"Never too late to try," she told him as cheerfully as she could. It was a philosophy she held dear to her own heart, but right now, given her present state, it lacked conviction.

He stopped mid-nod as another thought hit him. "But then who'd help you?"

"I'd be lost without you."

Pretending to be resigned, Gordon nodded, smiling to himself. "Nice to know."

"Hey, I'd always be lost without you," she told him firmly.

Philippe was right, Janice thought grudgingly as she walked into her bedroom and closed the door behind her. The faint scent of vanilla wafted to her, coming from yesterday's pile of folded laundry that she hadn't put away yet. Her brother needed to build up his self-esteem before he could be expected to fly.

Okay, so she owed Philippe, she told herself. She'd never liked owing anyone, even people she liked. She was going to have to find a way to settle up in the near future. But right now, she needed to get some sleep if she intended to be of any use tomorrow morning.

She slept fitfully, dreaming of a man with green eyes, a magnetic smile and hair the color of the heart of midnight.

They fell into a routine, despite the fact that every day brought new challenges, new work. The routine entailed that she and Gordon, with Kelli in tow, would show up at Philippe's doorstep each morning at exactly seven. Once Kelli was set up with either her easel or a book, she and Gordon would get down to work. They kept at whatever needed doing for the better part of four hours.

More than once, she'd pass by and catch Philippe admiring Kelli's work or giving the little girl pointers regarding her art. He was also the one Kelli turned to when she couldn't sound out a word. Hungry for a father figure, Kelli quickly transferred her affections to Philippe, lapping up any attention he gave her like a hungry puppy.

Janice noted that unlike the first few days, Philippe now kept his office door open. And as likely as not, Kelli would wander in to ask a question or offer an opinion about what she saw on his computer monitor. Or just to talk. And Philippe, Kelli told them proudly over meals, would always stop whatever he was doing to listen to her.

At around eleven, she and Gordon would break for lunch. Left on her own, she would work longer, but her brother tended to flag after four hours, needing to replenish his energy. Most of the time, Philippe would join them.

That had been her doing, inviting him to sample some of the food she'd brought with her in what Kelli referred to as "Mama's picnic basket." After a while, Philippe didn't need inviting, he just joined them when eleven rolled around, to sit and eat and talk amid the dust and the debris.

At times she'd just pull back and observe what was going on, as if she wasn't part of it. It always warmed her heart and, most of all, made her wish that things wouldn't end.

Because in this present framework, she could tell herself that she wasn't falling for the man, wasn't risking too much. After Gary had died she'd sworn never to put herself out there again, never expose her heart. Crushed again. Her parents and Gary had all left her in one way or another. She refused to endure that feeling of loss again.

But each time their hands accidentally touched, or she saw Philippe take time from his incredibly busy schedule to share a moment with her daughter, she felt something. Something strong. A pull that drew her directly to him—and made her dream, wishing things were different. Wishing she weren't afraid.

But she was and it was fear she hid behind.

Philippe had asked her out several times now and each time she'd made polite excuses—just strongly enough to hold him at bay, not strongly enough to rebuff him.

What the hell was she doing? she silently demanded of herself more than once. He was going to get tired of hearing excuses and stop asking. And that, she knew, was for the best.

And yet—

And yet she didn't want him to stop asking. Didn't want him to back away.

You don't know what you want, she admonished herself. And it was true.

"You're playing games, J.D. Never knew you to play games before," Gordon commented right after lunch one day. They'd been on the job for five weeks. Philippe had gone back to his office and she was clearing away the empty pizza box.

Overhearing, Kelli was quick to come to her defense. "Mama plays lots of games."

Janice offered her daughter what she hoped was an innocent, approving smile before turning to Gordon. "We'll talk about this later."

Gordon shook his head. "I'm not the one you should be talking to." The look he gave her was pregnant with meaning. And just in case she missed it, he indicated Philippe's office with his eyes.

Before she had a chance to tell her brother that none of this was any of his business, the front door suddenly opened. Lily sailed in majestically, taking the room— and attention—as if it rightfully belonged only to her.

The second the artist entered, Kelli abandoned her easel and raced to Lily as if the woman was a favorite aunt. Or a beloved grandmother. Neither of which she had.

Rather than just fluff her off, Lily got down to the little girl's level and put her arms around her. The hug was both warm and genuine and it was difficult to determine who enjoyed it more, the woman or the child.

"Hello, everyone," Lily declared in her clear theatrical voice as she regained her feet again. She looked directly at Gordon and then at her. "Didn't mean to interrupt anything."

Janice saw the amused look on Philippe's face as he entered from the hallway. He leaned against one wall, folding his arms before him. She had a feeling that they were both thinking the same thing: that it was a lie. Lily Moreau liked nothing more than making a grand entrance and bringing everything to a grinding halt by her mere presence. The woman clearly thrived on the spotlight, even if it was only the kind cast by a child's flashlight.

Chapter Twelve

"So, you are coming, aren't you?" Still holding on to Kelli's hand, Lily looked at her son expectantly, waiting for a confirmation.

"I might," Philippe allowed. "If I knew what you were referring to."

With an audible sigh, Lily shook her head, her chandelier earrings swaying rhythmically to and fro about her perfectly sculpted cheekbones. She slanted a mock exasperated glance toward Janice.

"Men. They never seem to retain anything in their heads except for a woman's measurements." She sighed again, her attention returning to Philippe. "To my opening, of course."

He pretended to consider her words carefully. "Didn't I already go to it?"

This time, the note of exasperation was genuine. "No, you didn't already go to it—because it was postponed." She waved a bejeweled hand dismissively, as if things only happened to either impede or enhance her daily life. "Something about the gallery owner coming down with a colossal case of gastritis or some such ailment. In any event, he closed down the gallery for two weeks." She frowned at such sacrilege. "In my day, you sucked it up for art and soldiered on."

Philippe grinned. "Especially for a Lily Moreau showing."

"Exactly." And then her turquoise eyes swept over the two other adults in the partially reconstructed room. "You're welcomed to come, too." She paused for a moment, looking at the coveralls that Janice was wearing. "But it is formal."

Janice never cracked a smile as she glanced down at the faded blue denim. "I guess that means I get to wear my strapless overalls."

Lily surprised her by taking it in stride. "Very funny, dear." The woman studied her torso, circling once before nodding. "I have clothes I can lend you." She turned to her son. "You can bring her to the house, Philippe. Give her anything she wants."

Panic pricked at Janice's belly. This was getting way too personal, too social. Her first reaction was to back away, to withdraw before there were consequences. "No, wait, I really don't think I can—"

But Kelli was already tugging on her arm. One look at the small, upturned face and Janice knew what was in her daughter's heart. "Please, Mama?"

"Yes, 'please Mama,'" Lily echoed for good measure, never once assuming that it would be any other way than how she wanted it to be. "It'll be good for the child," she assured Janice. "She should have exposure to the arts."

Janice could feel her back going up. She didn't welcome advice when none was requested, especially not when it came to Kelli. "I take her to the museum," Janice countered.

Lily was obviously unimpressed. "The visual arts," she emphasized. She looked down at Kelli with tremendous approval. "You're never too young to learn what the field is all about if you're going to make a living in it."

"She hasn't entered kindergarten yet," Janice pointed out evenly. "I think it's a little early to start giving her vocational guidance."

It was evident that Lily was not of the same opinion. "She has a gift, dear," the older woman told her kindly, patting her cheek. "You shouldn't keep it from the world—or the world from her, for that matter." Lily opened her purse and took out a mauve-colored card with the gallery's name on it. She pressed it into Kelli's hand. "Bring your mommy along. If she doesn't want to come, Philippe can bring you along with him."

It still amazed Philippe that his mother never thought that people might have other plans, plans that differed from hers.

He moved closer to Janice. "That's called kidnapping in some states, Mother."

Rings glinted in the sunlight as Lily waved a hand at him. There were times he wondered if she would be able to speak if her hands were tied. "Don't be so dramatic, Philippe. Honestly," she said to Gordon, "I don't know where he gets it from." She paused, the stranger's face finally registering in her brain. Always intrigued by a good-looking man, she abruptly asked, "And you are?"

"Really fascinated," Gordon responded. He seemed overcome by this vibrant and flamboyant woman.

Without realizing it, Gordon had chosen his words perfectly. Lily smiled broadly and the years instantly melted away. She presented him with her hand. It took him a second before he came to and shook it. "Well, Really Fascinated, I hope you have the opportunity to come to the opening, too."

And then it was time to go. Lily turned to Philippe. "Tomorrow night. Don't forget. The showing begins at eight. Try not to be late." Her sweeping glance took them all in just before she crossed to the front door. "Any of you."

"Can we go, Mama? Can we?" Kelli asked eagerly the moment Lily had left the house. She clutched at her mother's hand with both of hers, fairly dancing back and forth.

"Honey, that's a little late for you."

"I'll take a nap," Kelli told her, her eyes wide with innocence. "A long one. I promise."

Janice sighed. She was really reluctant to go, but it was hard saying no to Kelli. "We'll see."

"I can pick you up," Philippe volunteered. "That way, you won't have to worry about trying to locate the gallery in the dark."

Janice lifted her chin, instantly defensive after a lifetime of having to prove herself over and over again—and never being found good enough. "I have a very good sense of direction, thank you. I can find my own way to—" She paused to look down at the name on the card she'd taken from Kelli. "Sunset Galleries."

Philippe smiled, reading between the lines. "Then you'll come."

Damn it, she hadn't meant to imply that. Janice back-tracked. "Maybe."

"Mama," Kelli wailed, a pleading note in her high voice.

"Maybe," Janice repeated firmly, refusing to be pinned down or cornered by this handsome man or his larger-than-life mother.

On his way back to work in the kitchen, Gordon purposely walked by Philippe. He lowered his voice.

"She'll come. She's a pushover for Kelli even if she tries to come off tough."

Janice fisted her hands at her waist, the personification of feistiness. "I still have my hearing, Gordon."

Gordon turned around and grinned. "Never doubted it for a minute, J.D."

"I'm sorry about my mother," Philippe apologized to her as Gordon left the room. "She tends to be a little overbearing."

Now there was an understatement if she'd ever heard one. "You think?"

Over the years, he'd ceased being embarrassed by his mother's actions and had made a concentrated effort to understand her, to know the woman behind the dramatics. "But that's only because she cares so passionately. And she really does think that Kelli," he ran his hand over the little girl's silky hair, "shows a great deal of promise. I do, too. I don't have nearly the eye that my mother does, but I've never seen that kind of ability in someone so young. And in her own way, my mother's right. Exposure to an art gallery might be good for Kelli."

Janice stuck to her guns. Kelli was still four, not a junior in high school. "It's past her bedtime."

He spoke as someone who'd never had an enforced bedtime. "Kids are flexible."

She tried to summon indignation and found it was more difficult when she tried to mount it against him. Something about Philippe Zabelle disarmed her. Which frightened the hell out of her. "And you would know this how?"

The grin all but torpedoed her gut. "I put in my time as a kid. You'd be surprised what a kid can be capable of if the need arises."

She had a feeling he wasn't talking about staying up past a designated bedtime. In his own way, Philippe'd had as unorthodox a childhood as her own. Maybe even more so.

"We'll see," she repeated for the umpteenth time. "Kelli," she instructed, "go back to your drawing. As for me, I have work to do," she told Philippe. "You're not paying me to stand around and grow roots."

There was that grin again. Was it her imagination, or was he doing that a lot more lately? "I would if I could get to watch you do that."

She waved her hand at him as she turned away. But, walking into the kitchen, it was hard to keep her mouth from curving into a smile.

"Timing something?" Alain asked as he saw Philippe look at his watch for what had to be the fifth time in a very short interval.

Philippe dropped his hand to his side. "Just wondering where Mother is," he lied.

Alain grinned. "Well, Mother is probably waiting to make an entrance." He glanced toward the doorway. "You know how she is."

"He's waiting for the little fixer-upper to show," Georges interjected just before he took another sip from the glass of champagne he was husbanding. Two were his limit even though he had an evening off from the hospital. There was always a chance he'd be summoned and he liked being in control of his faculties.

Alain looked mildly surprised. His question was directed to Georges rather than Philippe. "The Wyatt woman is coming?"

Georges nodded, his attention temporarily captured by a canapé he'd snared from a passing waiter's tray. "Mother thinks her daughter has possibilities. Big brother, on the other hand," he inclined his head toward Philippe, "thinks that *she* might have possibilities." Turning toward Philippe, his train of thought halted. "Wow, did you know that you look like thunderbolts could come shooting out of your eyes? Easy, Philippe," he placed a soothing hand on his brother's shoulder, "I think this is a good thing. I haven't seen you interested in anything but a page of code for God only knows how long. Alain and I were beginning to worry about you."

He loved his brothers, but his personal life was his own. "You go out with enough women to make up for the rest of the family," Philippe pointed out.

"Hey, speak for yourself," Alain protested. "I need my own supply of women to keep me going." He grew just a tad serious. "And we're both glad that your interest's finally aroused."

He didn't mind being teased, but they had hit a sensitive spot. "What the hell do you know about my interest?" Philippe challenged. Up until this moment, he'd been fairly secure of his discretion when it came to Janice.

"They're called eyes, Philippe. Alain and I both have them and we use them on occasion," Georges told him, quickly picking up another canapé before the waiter made his way to the other end of the gallery. "We saw you at the poker game that night," he reminded Philippe. "You came to life when she showed up."

He hadn't behaved any differently before or after she'd arrived. Georges didn't know what the hell he was talking about. "You had too much beer."

"I *never* have too much beer," Georges told him. "And besides, it was the beginning of the evening."

Philippe refused to admit to anything. Not until he decided where he wanted this to go and *if* it was going to go anywhere. "Well, something definitely inhibited your perception."

"Denial is a sad thing to witness in a grown man," Alain pronounced before he took a long sip of his champagne. Georges was driving him home so he had no worries about needing to keep a clear head and, sometimes, his mother's shows were better endured just this side of inebriated.

"Speaking of grown men," Philippe neatly diverted the conversation away from himself, "how long do you think it'll take that one to reach maturity?" He nodded toward the young man who had entered the gallery with their mother on his arm.

"Long," Georges murmured, shaking his head.

This was a new face on him. "Who is he?" Philippe wanted to know.

"Mother's newest boy toy," Alain replied with resignation.

"Emphasis on *boy*," Georges chimed in.

Somewhat stunned, Philippe looked from the handsome baby-faced escort in the formal tuxedo to his brothers. "You're kidding."

"If only," Alain murmured.

"What cradle do you suppose darling Lily found him in?" Georges asked. Absently, he took another sip of champagne.

"Barely-legal-lovers 'R' Us?" Alain guessed.

Philippe frowned. They were making jokes, but this could be serious. Just how old was this newest interest of their mother? Of the three of them, he'd been the one who'd paid the most attention to the men who had paraded in and out of Lily's life. In the early days, some had been old enough to collect social security checks. Gradually, a trend took over. As his mother grew older, her lovers grew younger. For a while, her men had been the same age as she was. But in the last few years, they'd been younger. This one, however, was the first who looked as if he might be young enough to be her son.

"What the hell is she thinking?" Philippe asked.

Georges made a calculated guess. "Probably that the male of the species peaks at around nineteen while the average female hits her peak somewhere in her late thirties."

"Nothing average about our mother," Alain commented, watching the duo make their way into the center of the gallery.

Philippe shook his head. "Wouldn't it be nice if there were?"

Georges laughed. "Yes, but then she wouldn't be Lily Moreau, would she?"

"C'mon," Alain urged, setting down his empty glass on the edge of a table. "We might as well meet this one before the poor slob becomes history like all the others she's put through the mill."

Philippe hung back for a minute. Alain's words had more than a little truth to them. "Why bother, then?"

"Because she's Mother," Georges answered. "And underneath all that flamboyance is a very insecure creature who needs as much of our support as we can give her."

Philippe looked at him in surprise. "You really were paying attention in medical school."

Georges laughed. "Seemed like the thing to do at the time."

Philippe trailed after his brothers to greet not only his mother, who by now was the center of attention, but Kyle Autumn, the young man who looked remarkably comfortable and at home with all this commotion.

But just before he reached the outer circle around his mother, something out of the corner of his eye caught his attention.

Automatically glancing in that direction, he froze, his mouth threatening to fall open like some cardboard rendition of a Venus flytrap.

He recognized Kelli first.

There was no missing the bright, animated face even though she wore a deep green velvet dress instead of her customary overalls and pullover shirt.

The woman with Kelli, however, took his breath away and seriously threatened to short-circuit his brain. In one heartbeat he realized who she was.

The honey-blond hair was piled up high on her head, held there by fairy dust, magic and, he later discovered, a couple of strategically placed pins. Like the child she ushered in before her, the woman wore a dress. A dress that captured every bit of artificial light within its silvery threads, casting thin, gleaming rays that preceded her. Formfitting, it adhered seamlessly to her body from beneath her bare shoulders to the tips of her toes.

She moved like shimmering poetry.

Philippe found himself sincerely wishing that he could remember a line or two of verse that would begin to do her justice.

Wow seemed woefully inadequate somehow, but that was the only word that reached his lips, emerging in a soft, worshipful whisper.

"Wow."

Not quite sure if Philippe had said something or if he was imagining it, Georges turned first toward his brother, then in the direction that his brother was looking to see what had caught Philippe's attention so securely.

Once he did, a low, appreciative whistle escaped Georges's lips as pure admiration slipped over his chiseled features.

"Talk about cleaning up well," Georges muttered under his breath, watching the woman make her way into the gallery. He clapped his brother heartily on the back and declared with sincerity, "Philippe, I think you have a keeper there."

Only vaguely aware of what Georges was saying, Philippe began making his way over to Janice on legs that felt oddly spongy.

"You came," he said when he reached her, not bothering to hide either his surprise or his pleasure.

In response, a somewhat self-conscious smile worked its way across her lips and then faded a little. She wasn't used to dressing up anymore. It almost felt as if she had on her mother's clothes—if her mother had left any behind for her to wear. This definitely wasn't something that she'd have hanging in her closet under normal circumstances. But after Lily's comment about lending her suitable attire for the opening, she knew she had to find something that would knock the pins out from under the woman.

And if, perchance, the gown managed to do the same with Philippe, well, there was no harm in that, was there?

"Looks that way," she murmured, more pleased than she knew she should be by the look she saw on Philippe's face.

"I came, too," Kelli declared, underscoring her announcement with a firm tug on his sleeve.

There was warmth in his voice when he spoke to her. "So you did."

Bending down, Philippe picked the little girl up and was rewarded with a deep giggle and a hug. He returned the latter, then set her down again.

Try as he might, he couldn't seem to take his eyes off Janice. Because he didn't want to come off like a tongue-tied dolt, he said the first thing that came to his mind.

He repeated what Georges had said. "You clean up very well."

For a moment, she said nothing and he wondered if he'd somehow managed to insult her.

And then he saw her smile.

He wore a tuxedo, Janice noted, as did his brothers. She'd seen them first while secretly scanning the room for Philippe. Undoubtedly the tuxedos were at their mother's insistence. She had to admit that she found it rather sweet that the grown men loved their mother enough to humor her.

His brothers were good-looking in their attire, but

Philippe surpassed that. She found him breathtakingly handsome.

As if he needed any help to look that way.

"You, too," she murmured.

Chapter Thirteen

"She's getting too heavy for you," Janice protested to Philippe for the second time in the space of half an hour.

She, Gordon and Kelli had been there for almost three hours. For over half that time, Philippe had been carrying around a sleeping Kelli in his arms. Gordon had made himself scarce within ten minutes of their arrival, but Philippe had remained with them the entire time and Kelli had lit up like a Christmas tree whenever he spoke to her. As the little girl finally began losing her battle against drooping eyelids, he had picked her up. Kelli had been absolutely ecstatic, until she fell asleep.

But this, Janice thought, was above and beyond the

call. Despite the fact that watching him with her daughter tugged on her heart in the best possible way, she felt guilty for putting him out like this. He should be free to mingle—without a small girl in his arms.

Although she put her arms out to take her daughter, Philippe made no move to surrender his soft load to her. Instead, he merely shook his head, trying to put her concern to rest.

"I might not be a body builder," he told her, his voice low in order not to wake Kelli, "but the day I can't carry around forty pounds of sugar and spice without wheezing, I'm really in trouble. Besides," he added with a dazzling smile, "as long as I have your daughter, you can't leave."

Why was it every time she was on the receiving end of one of his smiles, something fluttered in her stomach? She was a grown woman, not some starry-eyed teenager. Reactions like that should have been long in her past.

But they weren't.

"So this is a hostage situation?" she asked wryly.

He liked bantering with her. Liked everything about her. The one exception was the very real threat to his peace of mind that she posed. But he was learning to deal with that.

"Something like that," he acknowledged. "It's working, isn't it?"

She laughed. Attending the show had been fun, but it was time for Cinderella to take her glass slippers and her coach and get home before she wore out her supply of fairy dust and midnight arrived. "Really, I think it's time I got her into bed."

Funny, the same thought had been crossing his mind. But it had nothing to do with the little girl he was carrying and everything to do with the woman whose presence made him forget the rules he'd so carefully laid down for himself.

Philippe watched her for a long moment. So long that it felt as if time had suddenly stood still. And all the while, he was debating the wisdom of what he was going to say next.

Wise or not, he couldn't stop the words. Couldn't annihilate the tiny slivers of desire that prompted him to speak.

"Far be it from me to interfere with motherhood, but could I interest you in stopping by my place for a nightcap? It's on the way," he added in case she was going to say something about wanting to go straight home.

"No. Really. Kelli. Bed." The words came out in staccato cadence as Janice allowed herself, for one moment, to entertain the idea of taking Philippe up on his offer.

And the offer she was certain lay beyond that.

It was a struggle, but she had to remain focused. She wasn't going to get involved, at least, not any further than she already was. It wasn't too late yet. The hook, the line, the sinker, they were all still within her grasp. But only if she backed away.

"You might be familiar with my place," Philippe continued as if she hadn't tried to protest. "It has extra bedrooms. The princess," he smiled at the bundle in his arms, who stirred, wrapped one small arm around his neck and went on sleeping, "is welcome to use any one of them."

Janice shifted so that her back was to the open room, creating a small, intimate pocket for herself, Philippe and her daughter. She tried not to dwell on just how intimate. "If Kelli's not in her own bed when she wakes up, she has a tendency to get scared."

"Really." He tried to look down at the face resting on his shoulder. Compassion nudged at him. He could remember Alain being abnormally afraid of the dark and Georges not being able to sleep unless the closet door was completely closed. "And I thought she was fearless."

Janice laughed softly. Kelli came off like gangbusters sometimes, but she was still a little girl, susceptible to the pitfalls of a vivid imagination. "We all have our quirks."

"Yes, we do. All right, if I can't talk you out of leaving, Cinderella, let me carry the crown princess to your car for you." When she began to protest yet again, he cut her short. "I've grown accustomed to the weight and it's a little hard to relinquish."

Janice smiled, running her hand along Kelli's head. The ribbon the little girl had insisted she put in her hair had come undone and was now drooping as much as she was. "I know the feeling." Raising her head, Janice's eyes met his. Something warm undulated through her, born of an unexpected communion and the surge of bitter-sweetness that she experienced seeing him holding her daughter like that.

The words seemed to come of their own volition. "You can come to my place."

He was almost certain he hadn't heard correctly. "Excuse me?"

Bail out. Say nothing, *and run for your life.* And yet, when she did speak, what emerged was none of that. "For that nightcap. If you'd still like to have one, you can come over to my place if you'd like."

The smile burrowed right through all the protective layers she'd ever constructed around herself. "I'd like," he said softly.

Nerves began jumping around like a compass placed in a field of magnets, warning her that she'd just taken a step into less than solid territory.

Reinforcements, she needed reinforcements, Janice thought, suddenly glancing around as she began leading the way to the front door.

"Looking for Gordon?" Philippe guessed, bringing up the rear.

She'd bailed him out so many times, it was time for him to return the favor. "I just want to tell him we're leaving."

But Gordon, it turned out, wasn't quite ready to go. He was having much too good a time. Mainly with the redhead he'd been monopolizing from the first hour he'd arrived.

Excusing himself for a moment, Gordon stepped over to the side to talk to Janice. "I'm going to hang around for a little while longer," he told his sister, then. Glancing over his shoulder toward the redhead, he added, "Don't wait up."

She knew that look. That was Gordon, smitten to the nth degree. Concerns immediately sprang up. Janice forgot that she was the one who needed help. "Gordon—"

A feeling of déjà vu washed over Philippe. This was an uncomfortable situation in the making, just the way it had been when his brothers used to go at one another when they were growing up. Time to stop it before it started.

"—Is a grown man, Janice. He's allowed to stay out late if he wants to," he pointed out.

Not expecting him to interfere, she looked at Philippe, stunned and, for the moment, speechless.

Gordon took advantage of the momentary respite and moved back to the redhead. But not before nodding his thanks to Philippe.

She supposed that Philippe was right. Gordon was a grown man, even if he didn't often behave like one. But still...

She shook her head as she started walking again. "He's only going to get hurt."

Well, at least she was talking to him, Philippe

thought. His little errand of mercy hadn't cost him that. "Maybe not. That's Electra," he told her.

They were outside now. The sky was studded with stars as she made her way to the back of the building and the parking lot where she'd left her car. "Beyond being the name of a heroine in some Greek play, is that supposed to mean something to me?"

"No, not to you," he agreed, "but to me. She's a distant cousin of Alain's—and a very nice girl," he added, hoping that would put her mind at ease.

"A distant cousin of Alain's," she repeated, stopping beside her car, "but not yours."

"No, not mine."

She began to look for her car key. For a small purse, it certainly didn't make the search easier. "And he's never been married?"

"No."

She took out her wallet and her cell phone. Holding both in one hand, she continued feeling around the bottom of the purse. "Then it's not possible."

"It is if Alain had a different father than I did."

She stopped looking. Her eyes raised to his. "Oh."

Now that he'd opened that door, he might as well open it all the way, Philippe decided. After all, it wasn't anything he was ashamed of, just something he didn't advertise. It made his mother seem inconstant—which she was but that was their business. However, something about this woman with the large soulful eyes made him want to share, to open all the doors and windows and air out the musty places that had known only darkness. "Georges did, too."

"Georges and Alain had a different father than you," she said out loud, trying to get it straight in her head.

"Why don't we take my car?" he suggested. "That way, Gordon won't be stranded. We can move the car seat," he added before she could protest.

"Okay." Opening the rear passenger door, she took out Kelli's car seat and followed behind Philippe to his sedan.

Philippe unlocked the passenger door of his car. "Fathers," he said, emphasizing the *S*. She looked at him sharply. "Different fathers." He wondered what she was thinking as she attached the car seat and then took her daughter from him, strapping Kelli in. "Mother got around," he commented philosophically. "And, apparently," he rounded the hood and got in on the driver's side, "it seems that nothing has changed in that department."

Janice pulled the seat belt around her, slipping the metal tongue into the slot. "You must have had a really rocky childhood." There was sympathy in her voice. Or was that empathy?

Either way, Philippe shrugged casually. "It was…interesting," he finally said, settling on a neutral word. He put his key into the ignition, turned it, then glanced behind him to see how Kelli was doing. She was still very soundly asleep. Like Alain at that age, he thought. He turned back around. "So, with your backup bailing out, I guess you'd rather I took a rain check on that nightcap." The car began to move.

Her sense of survival urged her to take the way out Philippe had just offered her.

But there was also her sense of competitiveness to reckon with, that edge that she'd always grasped in her struggle to make her an equal in a man's world.

She slanted a glance toward him. Philippe probably thought she was afraid of him. Nothing could have been further from the truth. If she was afraid of anything, it was herself.

Because of the feelings that had surfaced, hard and strong.

"Why?" she challenged him.

He smiled at her then, getting the very distinct impression that they were, in their own way, battling the same demon. The same fear, even if they had arrived at it by different routes.

He shrugged, easing out of the parking lot. "No reason."

Janice took a deep breath. She was going to regret this. She couldn't stop herself.

"All right, then," she said. "Make a left at the next light."

Philippe nodded, doing as she said. He refrained from telling her that he already knew where she lived. Because he'd always believed in covering all his bases.

* * *

She lived twenty minutes away, on the far end of Bedford. Because of Friday-night traffic, it took almost twice that amount of time to reach her house from the Lido Isle gallery.

Never one to care for driving, Philippe found himself enjoying the ride. They talked about Kelli and the show. Both seemed like safe enough topics.

She lived in one of the older developments within Bedford. But there was nothing old about the house. Even in the dark, with only the porch lights to guide him as he pulled up, the two-story dwelling looked as if it had just been renovated.

Renovated inside as well as out, Philippe noted as he carried the sleeping child into the house behind Janice. She'd tried to take Kelli out of the car seat, but he had gently moved her out of the way and done it himself. He'd pointed out that she was going to need at least one hand to hold up the edge of her gown when she negotiated the stairs. Reluctantly, she'd agreed, thinking him to be an unusually observant, sensitive man.

As if he needed more points.

"Really nice place you have here," Philippe said, looking around as he followed her. He made no attempt to hide his admiration.

There were no edges in sight, no angles, other than

the windows. The walls were all rounded and the rooms fed into one another via arched entrances.

Maybe he could stand to have more work done on his house, he thought.

"Did you do this all yourself?" The place suited her, all curves and rounded shapes.

She was surprised that he was giving her all the credit. After all, she'd told him that her father had been a contractor and there was Gordon who was more than capable, once he had a fire lit under him. Philippe wasn't trying to flatter her, she realized, he was serious.

"Mostly," she admitted, doing her best not to smile smugly. Her father and Gordon were traditionalists. She'd once dreamed of being an architect.

"You're better than I thought you were—" He turned to look at her. "And that's pretty damn good," he was quick to add, knowing how sensitive she could be.

Almost embarrassed despite the surge of pride that filled her, Janice changed the subject and nodded toward the stairs.

"This way." Taking hold of her dress, she raised it and led the way quickly.

Kelli's bedroom was the second door to the left. When she opened it, Philippe stood in the doorway, awed. There were murals on three sides of the room.

Kelli was one lucky little girl, he thought. "God, this is a child's fantasy come to life."

"She helped design it," Janice told him proudly. "And she painted that one."

She pointed out the pastoral scene on the right. That hand had been a little unsteady, but it was still very impressive, Philippe thought.

He placed Kelli down on a bed shaped like a tiny Viking boat. Fairies danced on the wall behind it, all appearing to gaze down at the little girl. Sweet dreams took on a new meaning.

Removing Kelli's shoes slowly, Janice threw a light sheet over her.

He'd just assumed that bedtime would have rituals attached to it. This was almost bohemian—something his mother would have approved of. "Aren't you going to change her?"

After pausing to switch on an oversized nightlight in the shape of a teddy bear, Janice began to back out of the room. She shook her head in response to his question. "You'd be surprised how that would wake her up. I can always wash her clothes."

Though a simple sentence, she had trouble getting it out. Her lips and throat were dry, in direct contrast to her hands, which felt damp.

This was ridiculous.

She couldn't seem to talk herself out of it.

Slipping out of the room, Janice took a deep breath as she closed the door. Then, summoning courage, she glanced up at him. "You don't really want a nightcap, do you?"

Philippe moved his head from side to side, his eyes never leaving hers. The temperature in the hallway rose several degrees of its own accord. "No."

Breathe, Janice. Breathe. Superhuman effort pushed more words out. "What do you want?"

He didn't answer her.

Instead, Philippe curved his fingers lightly along her face and brought his mouth down to hers. Slowly enough for her to pull away if she wanted to, quickly enough to steal away the breath she had just drawn in.

Janice was lost from the very beginning.

Maybe even from the moment she'd decided to come to Lily's showing. Because in her heart, as she slipped on the silvery gown, she knew it would end this way. Here, in a warm, intimate circle that included only the two of them, with emotions racing through her at the speed of newly charged lightning.

Being held, being kissed, being wanted, all of it hurt because of the inevitable disappointment that waited for her at the end of the road. But for the moment, for the very vibrant, pregnant moment, it felt beyond good. It felt absolutely wonderful.

Delicious.

And then, in a heartbeat, she found herself airborne. Philippe had swept her up in his arms.

"Where's your room?" he whispered against her temple, his breath feathering along her skin.

She was melting. Melting so quickly that for a second, she couldn't focus, couldn't think. It took effort to remember where she was. Or even who. And as for all the reasons this shouldn't be happening, she couldn't recall a single one.

"There," she finally managed, pointing to the door that stood across from Kelli's room. "There," she repeated urgently. Anticipation ran through her and every inch of her tingled.

Philippe moved the door open with his shoulder, carrying her into the room without drawing his mouth from hers.

Each kiss was deeper than the last.

Each kiss rendered her a little hotter, a little wilder than the one that had come before it. The eagerness frightened her even as it overwhelmed her. Not his but her own. When he set her back on the floor, a hunger took possession of her mind, her body, disintegrating the first, commandeering the second.

She all but tore away his jacket, his shirt, his trousers as her breath grew shallow and her desire grew deep.

"There's no zipper," Philippe realized in wonder. He drew back, catching her hands in his. "How—"

Swallowing, fairly certain that she was probably never going to be able to create saliva again, Janice took his long, artistic fingers and placed his hands on either side of the swell of her breasts.

"You tug." It was more of a seductive whisper than an instruction. "Slowly."

"Your idea of torture?" A smile rose to his lips as he obeyed.

About to answer, Janice jolted involuntarily as the material left her breasts. A shiver vaulted along her spine followed by a blast of heat. It was all she could do to keep from pushing him onto the bed. Where had this appetite, this hunger come from? How could she have not known of its existence? "Yours or mine?"

"Both," he whispered, stopping as the gown dipped just below her belly button, hugging her hips.

"What's wrong?" Why was he stopping? Had he changed his mind? Oh God, she'd fall to pieces if he changed his mind.

"Nothing." He groaned softly as he passed his hands over her breasts, her waist, her belly. "Not a single thing," he told her in a voice that was equal parts awe and worship.

He wanted this to last. He wanted her to remember. And he wanted to remember it as well. Not that there was any danger that it would get lost in a myriad of dalliances. He wasn't Georges or Alain.

But even so, he wanted this to be memorable for her.

So he kissed her. Over and over again. Kissed every part of her that was exposed to his gaze until he finally drew away the last of the material. It pooled like silver rain at her feet.

They tumbled onto her four-poster canopied bed, onto a comforter that felt more like a cloud than something meant to cover a bed.

And he began to make love to her in earnest, for all he was worth. As if he'd never made love to a woman before.

Because, as far as he was concerned, until this very moment, he hadn't.

Chapter Fourteen

Janice couldn't catch her breath.

Was it because, aside from that one mistake, she hadn't made love to anyone since Gary was killed?

Was it because, until Gary, she'd been a virgin and he had been her only actual partner, her only true lover? Was her admitted inexperience with lovemaking the reason why she now felt on fire?

The pleasure came at warp speed and she found herself peaking, one of the very few times she had attained a climax. And yet it wasn't over. There was so much more, wrapped up in agonizingly wonderful sensations. More than she'd ever realized there could be.

Philippe was an expert lover, yet she had no feeling that he was doing this by the numbers. Instead, it was if he was creating something new and wondrous just for her.

Janice moaned, wanting desperately to absorb every nuance, every sensation that went spinning through her. Absorb every pass of his hand, of his incredibly sensuous mouth.

She *had* to be dreaming. *Nothing* was this good and still real.

And yet…

He did things to her she'd never had done before, aroused her by skimming places no one had touched.

After she'd climaxed again, Philippe's tantalizing breath still warm on the sensitive skin just below her belly, she felt her heart pounding in her ears, the sound so loud it was almost deafening.

How did he do it? How did he manage to weave this magic, turning her into a mass of wants and needs? This wasn't her, had never been her. She was a rock.

She was pudding.

And what was she going to be like after it was all over?

Her heart still raced madly, and she was certain that it was trying to break out of her chest.

And then everything slipped into slow motion.

Philippe drew the length of his body over hers again. Two more heartbeats and he was over her. If her body wasn't already rivaling the physical composition of dissolved ice cream, she knew she would have melted all over again.

Damn him, he was making things happen, not just in her body, but in her heart. The latter both thrilled her and scared her to death. But if he stopped now, she'd die.

Janice arched her back, raising her hips up to him in heated surrender.

Instincts had always guided Philippe. He inherently knew just how to pleasure a woman. And that was important to him because pleasure was best mutually shared.

But this, this was different. *She* was different. Janice wasn't one of those high society women he was so accustomed to: beautiful women, all planes and angles and no substance. Those were women who felt that making love was just another part of life, no different than eating and sleeping, laughing and crying. Janice's hesitant eagerness, her unabashed enthusiastic response, stirred things within him, things he was unfamiliar with. Things he was almost afraid to examine.

A tenderness emerged along with a myriad of desires and passions and it gently elbowed its way forward. Stunning him.

He wanted her. Not wanted to make love, but wanted *her.* Wanted her within his days and in his nights.

This definitely put a different kind of light on everything.

He'd always been afraid of emulating his mother, of diving into a relationship and damning the consequences, stipulating that if a union didn't work, it could be easily dissolved. You didn't enter a relationship with both hands wrapped around a safety clause, holding on for dear life. You entered into it with dreams of forever.

Forever.

A word that had come to mean nothing to so many people. But it meant everything to him. The fear of not knowing how to get there was hard to shake. He had no example to follow.

He had only his heart.

Philippe held himself physically in check for as long as he could, then, as sweet agony ricocheted through his body when he drew it slowly along hers, he paused for a moment to look into her eyes. And then he entered her. Joining with her.

And stepping into something that had heretofore eluded him.

A feeling of belonging.

They were in-tune with one another from the moment he began the dance. With hips fitted together as if they'd been created that way, Philippe slowly increased the tempo. Increased it until he thought for sure he was going to explode.

Not a single cell within his body was unaffected when he achieved the final peak with her. Clasping the euphoria to him, he enveloped Janice in his arms and held her even closer.

Feeling her heart pounding against his was empowering yet humbling at the same time. And all the while, he felt a part of something. A part of her.

That had never happened before.

As the mists slowly parted and he found himself returning to earth, Philippe realized that he hadn't shifted his weight. He was probably crushing her.

Very gently, he moved from her. But rather than just claim his own section of her bed, he continued to hold her, united in spirit if not in body. All he heard was the sound of their breathing. And then he felt Janice shrinking from him, even though she hadn't actually moved.

Oh God, what have you done, Janice? What have you gone and done? She stared at the ceiling. "I guess you'll be wanting to go."

Philippe turned his head toward her. Go? He honestly hadn't thought that far ahead, but instead basked in the incredible feeling of contentment that had found him.

"Why?"

"Because…" She licked her lips. It didn't help. They remained drier than last year's paint chips. "Because you got what you came for."

The simple statement stunned him. Philippe rose up on his elbow and looked at her. "Is that what you think? That I 'came for' this? Like I was 'borrowing' a hammer or a cup of sugar?"

Pulling the edge of the comforter to her, covering up her nakedness, Janice sat up. She kept her face averted.

If she didn't see him, maybe she wouldn't burst into tears. Where *was* all this emotion coming from?

She sighed, tamping down the urge to pull the comforter over her head as well. "Look, I don't do this kind of thing."

She heard his soft laugh behind her. "Well, for a novice, you were incredible."

She stiffened, not taking the words as a compliment. She was too scared of what she was feeling and frantically tried to shut down. Completely. "I don't sleep around."

"I didn't say you did."

She felt his breath zipping along her bare back and struggled to turn herself into stone. "But you had to think it."

"Why?"

Why, why. Was he trying to bait her? Frustration surfaced. "Because you're here. Because we made love."

"And it was great," he agreed, "but why would that automatically mean that you slept around?"

Janice dropped her head against her knees. "You're confusing me."

"That makes two of us." She felt him tugging lightly at the comforter. Her fingers instantly clamped down on it. "I've just discovered this fantastic way to make your mind go blank."

She felt his fingertips playing along her spine, causing sensations she had no defenses against. Born moving, they zipped up and down her back. She took in a deep breath, struggling for the strength to resist. "Don't."

He leaned in against her, his cheek a fraction away from her spine. She both felt and heard the words. "Do you really mean that?"

Pulse points began to throb throughout her body. Janice turned around to face him, suddenly ravenous for him. How was that even remotely possible, given how exhausted she'd felt just two minutes ago?

"No," she whispered, her body aching for his. "No."

"Good answer," he said, pulling her to him.

Philippe captured her mouth, kissing her as if he hadn't just spent the better part of an hour making love with her. As if he were insatiable.

Because, he realized just before oblivion came for him, when it came to Janice, he was.

Janice stirred, her eyes fluttering against the infusion of light.

Daylight.

Morning!

She jerked up in bed, simultaneously realizing that she'd fallen asleep and trying to pull her thoughts together. She looked around frantically. What time was it?

Time to be alone.

The place beside her in the bed was empty.

The clothes that she'd all but ripped off his body, were gone.

Philippe had vanished.

He'd left, she thought, feeling a sharp pang in her gut.

Damn it, why was she feeling like this? She'd known he'd leave, that their night was a one-time thing. Why then—

Her train of thought stopped abruptly.

What was that smell?

Janice moved her head around, sniffing. Searching for the source. Her windows were closed, so the smell couldn't be coming from outside. That meant it was inside. She took another breath, a longer one this time. The smell was coming from downstairs.

Was something burning?

Kicking aside the comforter, she hit the floor moving. Janice grabbed a pair of jeans and a sweater, pulling them on as she ran down the hall. She needed to get to Kelli and to rouse Gordon—if he'd ever made it back home.

Her heart pounded, her brain processed a hundred different things at once until she realized she was smelling coffee and bacon.

The house wasn't on fire.

Sighing, momentarily drained, Janice leaned against the wall and dragged her hand through her hair. Was she still dreaming? No one made breakfast around here but her. That's the way it had always been, ever since her mother had taken off. Gordon was completely culinarily challenged and her father had only known how to make coffee and burn steaks.

What the hell was going on here?

Barefoot, she decided to go downstairs to investigate. But not without first arming herself. Gordon's door was standing open. He obviously hadn't come home for the night. His bed was still made and Gordon could no more make a bed than he could boil water.

Her brother still played softball on occasion and his bat was leaning against the wall next to the closet. Getting it, Janice went downstairs, her heart in her throat.

With both hands wrapped around the Louisville Slugger, she made her way to the kitchen, holding her breath and not knowing what to expect.

But it certainly wasn't what she saw: Philippe, his formal dress shirt hanging open, standing barefoot beside the stove, making breakfast.

The bat slid from her fingers.

Hearing the clatter, Philippe turned toward the doorway. His expression softened into amusement and he nodded at the fallen weapon. "You usually bring a bat to breakfast?"

Feeling foolish, she picked up the bat and retired it in the corner against the pantry. "I thought you were a burglar."

His amusement heightened. He went back to cracking eggs and watching over the bacon. "People often break into your house to make you breakfast?"

Very funny. Feeling somewhat self-conscious after last night, Janice did her best to brazen out the situation.

"Nobody makes me breakfast." She joined him at the stove. "Ever."

She reached for the frying pan, but he pushed her hand away. When she eyed him quizzically, he said, "You don't have to do everything, Janice."

She frowned, reluctantly taking a step back. "I'm not used to being served."

He nodded toward the stool at the counter, indicating that she should take a seat. "And I'm not used to having a woman wield a hammer, but they tell me it's a brave new world out there. No clear-cut roles, no black-and-white rules to follow." Finished, he transferred the scrambled eggs to a waiting plate and framed it with two strips of bacon. He placed the finished product in front of her. "Enjoy. I didn't poison it, I promise."

She took a breath and drew the plate in a little closer. "When did you learn how to cook?"

"When the nanny kept burning the oatmeal." He paused for a second, collecting various scattered fragments together. "Allison was her name, I think." He pictured the woman in his mind's eye. She'd been a great deal more formidable looking than his mother. The last one anyone would suspect of shirking her duties. "She kept a small bottle of scotch in her purse. Kept that purse pretty close to her as I remember. Go on," he urged again. "Try it."

Having no other recourse, feeling incredibly awkward about being served, Janice sank her fork into the eggs and then raised it to her lips. When she drew the fork out again, she forced a smile to her face.

"Good."

The forced smile had nothing to do with what she had just sampled and everything to do with what she was feeling. She was so confused she could hardly stand it.

Janice stared down at her fork for a second before moving it again. "I thought you'd gone," she said softly as she took another bite.

Nursing a cup of coffee he'd poured earlier, Philippe looked at her. The pinch of hurt he felt surprised him. "Did you think I'd leave without saying goodbye?"

Janice shrugged, still avoiding his eyes. "My mother did. It's easier that way."

"I don't usually take the easy way." He placed his hand over hers. When she still didn't look up, he crooked his finger beneath her chin and physically raised her head until her eyes met his. "Look, Janice, I don't exactly know what's going on here," he told her honestly. "But I'm willing to find out." He paused, searching her face. "How about you?"

The inside of her mouth went dry. Mercifully, she was spared having to give him an answer because Kelli, bless her, picked that exact moment to come running into the kitchen. The expression on her small heart-shaped face was one of surprise and pleasure at seeing Philippe standing there.

Within a moment, she was next to him, looking up as if he were the eighth wonder of the world—and all hers.

"What are you doing here?" Kelli asked, her voice sounding so grown-up he couldn't help laughing.

"Well, I was in the neighborhood," he told her, "and I thought I'd stop by and make you and your mommy breakfast."

Her eyes were huge. "Really?"

"Really," he told her solemnly.

She cocked her head, her eyes narrowing. "Why are you still wearing what you had on last night?"

Janice's heart sank, but Philippe never wavered. "I was in a hurry to make you breakfast. Take a look." Picking the little girl up with one arm, he brought her over to the stove. Besides the eggs he'd made for Janice and the bacon that still remained, there were waffles beginning to turn a golden color on the griddle.

Kelli seemed duly impressed. "Wow." She turned her head toward Philippe, her hair brushed against his cheek. "I thought only Mommy could make waffles."

"They're probably not as good," Philippe allowed gallantly as he brought her over to the counter, placing her on the stool beside Janice. "But you can tell me what you think." Taking them off the griddle, he slid the waffles onto a plate and then placed that before Kelli. A fork and napkin were beside the plate a second later. "Jam or syrup?" he asked formally, as if he were a food server waiting on her.

Was it her imagination or had Kelli sat up a little straighter just then? "Syrup, please."

Janice watched Philippe cross to the cupboard and reach in. "Syrup it is."

He moved around her kitchen as if he was more familiar with it than she was, she thought grudgingly. Worse, Philippe moved around her daughter as if he was more familiar with her than she was.

With no effort at all, he was making a niche for himself in her life. And with no effort at all, he could be gone just as quickly, she reminded herself darkly.

In the blink of an eye.

That was how her life always changed. Quickly. In the blink of an eye. One minute, she was standing in her yet unoccupied nursery, picking out curtains for the windows, and the next minute, there were two polite marines in dress uniforms, telling her the man whose child she was carrying wasn't coming home under his own power, but in a box.

She couldn't do that again. Couldn't just stand around, waiting to be devastated, waiting for her world to be blown apart.

She had to get away before that happened. Had to flee. The first chance she had. To save herself and Kelli.

Chapter Fifteen

Janice didn't show up. Not at seven. Not at eight. And not at nine.

After turning up like clockwork at his house every weekday for the last six weeks, neither Janice nor Gordon made an appearance at his door the following Monday morning.

He felt like his day couldn't start until he saw her face.

His deadline was drawing uncomfortably closer, but Philippe couldn't focus, couldn't pull his brain together long enough to make any sort of headway with the program additions he was creating. Every five, seven, ten minutes his thought process would break up and reform to include Janice and *only* Janice. A restlessness pervaded through him that grew more intense with every minute.

By nine-fifteen, Philippe had abandoned all attempts at concentration and called her twice. Twice and only gotten her voice mail, both on her landline and her cell phone. Each time he was urged to leave a message.

"If you're there, Janice, pick up," he instructed, then ordered, then supplicated. None of the approaches obtained him any sort of a response. Annoyed, he'd hung up.

Where the hell was she?

Why wasn't she here?

Had something happened? And if it had, why hadn't she called to say she'd be late or unavoidably detained or there tomorrow? At the very least, if she were caught up in something and unable for some reason to call, why hadn't Gordon called in her place?

Something was wrong.

He wasn't the type to let his imagination run away with him, never had been, but it was going the distance right now. He couldn't help it. The woman was nothing if not punctual and diligent. He'd never seen a work ethic like hers before. Everyone he'd ever known who'd had work done on his or her house, even those who had been supremely satisfied at the end, said that the crew was *never* there day after day, working. The norm was that, excellent or not, they would disappear for days at a time. Maybe even for a week or more.

But not Janice. Janice was always there, determined to see the job through to its completion. That was the first thing he'd liked about her.

Well, maybe not the first thing, Philippe amended, his pacing bringing him up to the front door again, but it had certainly been among the first.

He paused to look at the easel tucked away in the alcove. Paused to look at the small painting resting there. Intended, he knew, for him.

Maybe something had happened to Kelli, maybe that was why Janice hadn't called him, hadn't left any messages. He felt a chill pass over his spine. Something had happened to Kelli.

No, that couldn't be it. If something had happened to the little girl, Janice knew he'd be there for both of them. In a heartbeat. They'd gotten too close for him to be excluded.

Too close.

Yes, damn it, he'd gotten too close. Too close when before he'd kept life, kept women, even the ones he slept with, at a comfortable distance.

But before was when he hadn't found a woman he felt he wanted to spend the rest of his life with.

The thought, the *realization,* hit him right between the eyes.

Philippe slid onto the sofa without being completely conscious of what he was doing.

He *did* feel that way about her. Oh God, when had that happened? When had forever snuck in?

That was his mistake. That was why he felt like some wild, disoriented creature. Because he'd let down his walls and however unintentionally, allowed Janice to come through. Allowed himself to believe that forever was attainable.

He knew better than that. Why should he have better luck than his mother? His mother had always been in love with love, in love with the idea of being in love. She was more than willing to risk it all and what had it gotten her? A string of ex-spouses and broken relationships.

Did that mean that he was doomed to the same?

Philippe sprang to his feet as if someone had just shoved a hot poker into the cushion beneath him. He *wasn't* doomed to the same fate, not if he could help it. Not by a long shot.

Filled with new determination, pushing down any thoughts that didn't have to do with advertising pitches, Philippe strode back into his office and forced himself to focus on his work.

That lasted all of forty minutes. A new record for the day.

Why the hell was he even pretending? Philippe flipped open his cell phone and hit the button for Janice's cell.

Ten minutes, four attempts and twenty rings later, he flipped it closed again. It was time to take matters into his own hands. It was time to get some answers.

Two minutes later, he'd locked up his house and was in his car. Had he frightened her? he wondered as he drove to Janice's house. Had making love followed up by making breakfast somehow been too much for her? Cut into her space?

He knew Janice was her own person, that she valued her independence, but after the response he'd felt the night before, he thought she was ready to share that space just as she's shared her bed and her body.

Obviously, he must have thought wrong.

With effort, he forced himself to ease back on the gas pedal. He was going fifty-three miles an hour, eighteen miles over the speed limit in this particular section of the city.

God, if he *had* scared her off, he was prepared to back-track, to reconstruct all the collapsed bridges until they could sustain his weight as he crossed them to her again.

He was willing to do anything. Anything but say goodbye.

By the time Philippe arrived at her door, he'd gone back and forth in his mind so many times he felt like a worn-out tennis player.

He barely closed the door of his car, then hurried up the front walk. He didn't bother with the doorbell, but pounded on her door just the way Janice had on his when she'd come to drag her brother away from the poker table.

That seemed so long ago now. And yet, it hadn't

been. Everything that had happened had transpired in a very short time. Maybe that was the trouble....

Sick of second-guessing, Philippe pounded on the front door again.

This time, an incredibly sleepy-looking Gordon, attired in pajama bottoms and looking very much like an unmade bed, opened the door. Scrubbing one hand over his stubbled face, Gordon obviously tried to focus his eyes. He seemed to be hanging on to the door for support.

"Hey, man, do you know what time it is?"

Philippe walked in. "Do you?"

"Yes, it's—" Gordon blinked, seeing daylight streaming in behind Philippe. Still hanging on to the front door, he looked at the clock on the mantle. "Hey, wow, it's not six, is it?"

Philippe pivoted on his heel. "No, it's not six," he snapped, then made an attempt to rein in his temper. "Where's your sister?" Janice's truck, when he'd pulled up, hadn't been parked outside and the garage door was standing wide open, allowing him to see that the vehicle wasn't inside, either.

Gordon took a deep breath, as if that would somehow help to engage his brain. Releasing it, he shook his head, then dragged one hand through his hair.

"I dunno," he admitted. "She should have woken me up for work." He looked sheepishly at Philippe. "I hate the sound of an alarm clock."

Philippe could in no way process this personal piece

of information about the other man, not right now. Every cell in his body was focused on trying to find Janice. His fear threatened to explode at any second. "Did she say anything about getting a late start today?"

Gordon shook his head. "No."

Philippe tried again. "Did she say anything about buying more supplies?"

Again the shaggy head moved from side to side in denial. "No."

He was getting dangerously close to the end of his rope. "Did she—"

"No, no, no," Gordon declared, pulling both hands through his hair. "J.D. didn't say anything about anything. She was very quiet this weekend." He looked up suddenly at his visitor as the thought struck him. "Like she was right after she found out that Gary wasn't coming home." The thought sank in and Gordon looked at Philippe. "You two have a fight?"

"No." Philippe pressed his lips together. He wasn't the kind to share, not even with his brothers. So sharing personal information with someone who was almost a stranger to him was completely foreign. But at this point he was willing to try anything to help pull the pieces of the puzzle together. "It was just the opposite." He paused significantly, hoping Gordon was clever enough to pick up on what he was saying. "I thought everything was great."

Gordon seemed a little concerned himself. "Well,

obviously something wasn't so great," he theorized. "Otherwise, J.D. would have been in my room, kicking my butt at six and telling me to get the hell out of bed." Scratching his head, Gordon realized that he was talking to himself. Philippe had left the room.

Walking into the hall, he saw that the man was already halfway up the stairs. "She's not up there, man," Gordon called after him.

Philippe made no answer, just kept going.

Maybe there was something in Janice's room that would tell him where she'd gone.

Trying to calm himself, he silently insisted that he was probably just overreacting because he valued routine so much and she had broken hers.

He stopped dead in the doorway when he reached her room. The closet doors were standing open and it was obvious that a section of clothing was missing.

"This is bad," he heard Gordon say. The man was standing behind him.

Philippe turned around. "Why?" he demanded, even though he knew damn well that missing clothing and a missing woman did not add up to a good thing. He was hoping against hope that Gordon would say something he could hang on to.

But he didn't. "Because she took some of her things. And her suitcase is gone." Gordon pointed to a space on the floor.

Just as he did, Philippe noticed a folded up piece of

paper on the dresser. When he opened it, he saw that Janice had left a note for her brother. "Gordon," she wrote, "Kelli and I had to take off for a few days. Don't worry. Please finish up for me at the Zabelle place. Love, J.D."

The Zabelle place. As if there was nothing between them. As if he was nothing more than another job.

Philippe squelched the desire to crumple up the paper. Instead, he handed it to Gordon. "When was the last time your sister just took off like this?"

Gordon stared down at the note as if the words were not sinking in. "Never."

"Do you have any idea where she'd go?"

Gordon shook his head. "No." And then he stopped, his eyes widening as a thought hit him. "Wait." He turned toward Philippe. "Maybe. Maybe I do."

Philippe took a breath, waiting. He didn't care where it was, he was going to go after her and bring her back, even if it meant going to hell and back. "I'm listening."

Gordon ran his tongue nervously along his lower lip, afraid of making the wrong call. "She could have gone to the cabin."

"The cabin," Philippe echoed. When Gordon didn't elaborate further, he pushed, "What cabin?"

"When we were kids, my dad used to rent this cabin one week a year. It's up by Whitewood," he added, citing a resort area. "I always hated going there, but she loved it."

"Can you give me something more specific than a 'cabin in Whitewood?'"

Gordon thought a minute, as if his mind had gone completely blank. And then he looked up, a relieved smile on his lips. "Yeah."

"Good," Philippe retorted between closely clenched teeth.

Gordon made the next logical guess. "You going up there to get her?"

Again, it was against his nature to let anyone in. He'd grown up holding all his emotions close, not allowing the kind of hurt he'd privately viewed his mother enduring *ever* find him. That meant keeping everything damned up. But suddenly, it was just too late for that. And he was going to need allies. Gordon was her brother, that qualified him for the part.

So he looked at the other man and announced, "Damn straight I am."

Gordon grinned and nodded his approval. "My money's on you. Got a map in your car?"

Philippe was already on his way to get it.

It took Philippe the better part of the day to locate exactly where Janice had gone. Gordon's instructions only took him so far and no further. Apparently boyhood memories for Gordon were rather hazy.

Refusing to give up, Philippe backtracked to a general store he'd seen in the area. The clerk behind the counter told him the whereabouts of the local rental agency. Philippe left a ten in his wake and forgot to take the bottle of water he'd purchased.

Hadley's Rental Agency had been there almost as long as the mountains had. Joseph Hadley, the present owner, was a heavyset man who completely filled out the chair behind his desk.

He sat in it now, rocking back and regarding Philippe suspiciously as the latter asked him if a woman with a little girl in tow had rented a cabin in the last few hours.

"Don't give out information like that, son," he announced after a long, pregnant pause. "Violates a trust."

Philippe thought of trying to bribe the owner, but Hadley seemed like a man who valued his integrity and enjoyed letting everyone else know it.

Desperate, Philippe glanced at the small older woman who occupied the only other desk in the small office. She eyed him with a touch of curiosity that appeared to mingle with sympathy.

She could be won over, Philippe thought. But only for a price. With his back to the wall, Philippe again found himself in a position where he had to share his personal business and, more important, his feelings with a stranger.

With *strangers,* he amended silently, resigning himself to what he knew he had to do.

"I'm looking for my fiancée, Janice Wyatt. She just took off this morning without any explanation." She wasn't his fiancée, but if he had to go this far, he might as well embellish and go for broke. Whatever it took to find out where Janice had gone.

Hadley's tiny eyes all but disappeared as he moved forward on his chair and squinted. "You hit her?"

"No," Philippe declared with feeling, the very thought turning his stomach. "Never raised a hand—or my voice," he added for good measure. "Her first husband was killed in the war—"

It was all he needed to say. Mrs. Hadley's imagination—or intuition—filled in the rest. "Poor thing's probably afraid to take another chance on love. Heartache's a powerful deterrent."

The second the woman uttered the words, they hit home. Philippe, prepared to humor her, looked at Mrs. Hadley in awe instead. "You're right."

"Of course I'm right," the woman said with a nod. "Don't get to sit on this mountain, watching people for close to sixty-five years and not pick up a few things." She turned to her husband, "Give him the cabin number, Joe."

"Mary Beth, that's not the way we do business," her husband growled.

She waved a hand at him dismissively. "That's not the way you do business." Walking over to the large map of the area that covered the wall behind her husband's desk, she pointed out the cabin that had been rented last. "She's right there. Go out, take the road on the right and follow it until it disappears." She smiled at him. "That'll be the backyard. You can't miss it," she promised.

Philippe thanked them both and was back in his car in under a minute.

Twilight was just beginning to tiptoe down the mountainside as Philippe slowly made his way along the winding road and first spotted her. It had taken him a lot longer than he'd first thought, but the only thing that mattered was that he'd found her.

Janice was outside, playing a game of catch with her daughter.

A rather bad game of catch, Philippe noted, amused, as he parked his vehicle and made his way silently up the path.

Kelli threw the ball to her, but it fell right through Janice's hands. She was obviously preoccupied.

Not knowing what she was liable to do, he didn't speak until he was directly behind her. "You make a lousy catcher."

Janice caught her breath. Swinging around, she almost shrieked. She half expected him to be a fabrication of her overworked imagination. But Kelli saw him, too. Abandoning the game, she ran like a shot across the grounds and launched herself straight into his arms.

"You're here!" she cried at the top of her lungs, wrapping her arms around him. "You're here!"

He rose with her in his arms, thinking how incredibly

sweet it felt, holding her like this. As he basked in her blatant adoration, he felt his heart swell. "Yes," he told her, kissing the top of her head, "I am."

It took Janice a long moment to find first her breath, then her voice. "What are you doing here?" she managed to ask.

Holding Kelli to him, he turned to look at her. Well, at least she wasn't fleeing.

"Moving heaven and earth, looking for you," he told her without fanfare. And then, in case she didn't realize just what it had taken to find her, he added, "I had to spill my guts to complete strangers to find out where you got to. Do you have any idea how hard that was for me?"

Stunned, at a loss, she stared at him. "I—"

He didn't wait for her to respond, because there were more important questions to be answered. "Why did you suddenly go on the lam?" With effort, he kept his voice upbeat for Kelli's sake.

Janice raised her chin defiantly. "Gordon'll finish your bathrooms."

His eyes narrowed. His voice was low. "That's not what I asked."

Janice glanced toward the mountain range rather than at him. Because he had gone through all this effort to find her, she supposed she owed him the truth. "Because I didn't want to be hurt again."

The woman at the cabin had been right, he thought. "Well, that's good because I don't want to hurt you."

Gently, he set Kelli down and stepped into Janice's line of vision. "Go on," he urged. "So far we're on the same page."

She shrugged, feeling lost, feeling alone and feeling very angry at being cornered this way. Why couldn't he have just accepted things and let her go? Why did he have to put her through this?

"That's it."

"That's it," he repeated incredulously.

"That's it," she echoed. Her voice took on strength as she restated her reason. "I don't want to be hurt again."

He was going to get her to see the light if it killed him. Because suddenly nothing had ever been as important as this.

"Did it occur to you that maybe the solution to never hurting again is *not* not to love but to get the most out of the love that's possible?" he asked. When she began to turn away again, he caught her by the shoulder and continued. "To enjoy and savor each day as if there's no tomorrow and to keep doing it as long as tomorrow keeps coming?"

Janice blinked. She'd heard only one thing. One word. The word that ultimately was the most important one in the world. She needed him to repeat it, to explain. Because she was afraid she was imagining things, hearing what she wanted to hear. "What love? Who said anything about love?"

"He did, Mama," Kelli piped up helpfully, dramatically pointing to Philippe.

He grinned, first at Kelli, then at her. "What she said."

But Janice shook her head. This couldn't come via hearsay or second-hand repetition. "I don't want what she said, I want to hear what you said. Are you telling me that you love me?"

He looked as if it was a surprise to him, too. But not an unwelcome one. "Yes, I guess I am." Then, trying it on for size, he said it formally. "I love you, Janice Diane Wyatt."

"And me?" Kelli asked eagerly.

"And you, too." Philippe laughed, bending over and kissing the top of her head. And then, straightening, his eyes shifted to Janice's face. For just a second, he tried to pretend he was all business. "By the way, when you do get around to finishing my place, my brothers have some renovations they want you to handle on their houses. You up for that?"

When she stared at him numbly, apparently unable to decide if she was hallucinating, he took her in his arms. Just as she caught her breath, he kissed her. Once, and then again. Deeply and with feeling.

He heard her sigh against his lips.

"Yes," she murmured, answering a question that he had silently asked with his kiss.

"Yes, what?" he asked.

"Yes, I'll do the renovations." And then she smiled broadly. "And yes, I'll marry you."

Kelli looked up at her, perplexed. She tugged on her

mother's shirt. "But Mama, he didn't ask that," she pointed out.

Delighted, euphoric, Philippe laughed as he looked down at the little girl who was going to be his daughter. "Actually, I did. I asked her with my heart."

Kelli's eyes grew wide. She stared at him as if he were magical. "You can do that?"

Janice locked her hands along the back of his neck. "He can do that," she told her daughter just before the man she'd fallen in love with kissed her again, crushing the words, "I love you, too," against her lips.

* * * * *

Don't miss Marie Ferrarella's next novel,
DOCTOR IN THE HOUSE,
available September 2007
from Harlequin Next.

Welcome to cowboy country...

Turn the page for a sneak preview of
TEXAS BABY
by Kathleen O'Brien
An exciting new title from
Harlequin Superromance for everyone
who loves stories about the West.

Harlequin Superromance—
Where life and love weave together
in emotional and unforgettable ways.

CHAPTER ONE

CHASE TRANSFERRED his gaze to the road and identified a foreign spot on the horizon. A car. Almost half a mile away, where the straight, tree-lined drive met the public road. He could tell it was coming too fast, but judging the speed of a vehicle moving straight toward you was tricky.

It wasn't until it was about two hundred yards away that he realized the driver must be drunk…or crazy. Or both.

The guy was going maybe sixty. On a private drive, out here in ranch country, where kids or horses or tractors or stupid chickens might come darting out any minute, that was criminal. Chase straightened from his comfortable slouch and waved his hands.

"Slow down, you fool," he called out. He took the porch steps quickly and began walking fast down the driveway.

The car veered oddly, from one lane to another, then up onto the slight rise of the thick green spring grass. It just barely missed the fence.

"Slow down, damn it!"

He couldn't see the driver, and he didn't recognize this automobile. It was small and old, and couldn't have cost much even when it was new. It was probably white, but now it needed either a wash or a new paint job or both.

"Damn it, what's wrong with you?"

At the last minute, he had to jump away, because the idiot behind the wheel clearly wasn't going to turn to avoid a collision. He couldn't believe it. The car kept coming, finally slowing a little, but it was too late.

Still going about thirty miles an hour, it slammed into the large, white-brick pillar that marked the front boundaries of the house. The pillar wasn't going to give an inch, so the car had to. The front end folded up like a paper fan.

It seemed to take forever for the car to settle, as if the trauma happened in slow motion, reverberating from the front to the back of the car in ripples of destruction. The front windshield suddenly seemed to ice over with lethal bits of glassy frost. Then the side windows exploded.

The front driver's door wrenched open, as if the car wanted to expel its contents. Metal buckled hideously. Small pieces, like hubcaps and mirrors, skipped and ricocheted insanely across the oyster-shell driveway.

Finally, everything was still. Into the silence, a plume of steam shot up like a geyser, smelling of rust and heat. Its snake-like hiss almost smothered the low, agonized moan of the driver.

Chase's anger had disappeared. He didn't feel anything but a dull sense of disbelief. Things like this didn't happen in real life. Not in his life. Maybe the sun had actually put him to sleep....

But he was already kneeling beside the car. The driver was a woman. The frosty glass-ice of the windshield was dotted with small flecks of blood. She must have hit it with her head, because just below her hairline a red liquid was seeping out. He touched it. He tried to wipe it away before it reached her eyebrow, though, of course that made no sense at all. Her eyes were shut.

Was she conscious? Did he dare move her? Her dress was covered in glass, and the metal of the car was sticking out lethally in all the wrong places.

Then he remembered, with an intense relief, that every good medical man in the county was here, just behind the house, drinking his champagne. He found his phone and paged Trent.

The woman moaned again.

Alive, then. Thank God for that.

He saw Trent coming toward him, starting out at a lope, but quickly switching to a full run.

"Get Dr. Marchant," Chase called. "Don't bother with 911."

Trent didn't take long to assess the situation. A fraction of a second, and he began pulling out his cell phone and running toward the house.

The yelling seemed to have roused the woman. She opened her eyes. They were blue and clouded with pain and confusion.

"Chase," she said.

His breath stalled. His head pulled back. "What?"

Her only answer was another moan, and he wondered if he had imagined the word. He reached around her and put his arm behind her shoulders. She was tiny. Probably petite by nature, but surely way too thin. He could feel her shoulder blades pushing against her skin, as fragile as the wishbone in a turkey.

She seemed to have passed out, so he put his other arm under her knees and lifted her out. He tried to avoid the jagged metal, but her skirt caught on a piece and the tearing sound seemed to wake her again.

"No," she said. "Please."

"I'm just trying to help," he said. "It's going to be all right."

She seemed profoundly distressed. She wriggled in his arms, and she was so weak, like a broken bird. It made him feel too big and brutish. And intrusive. As if touching her this way, his bare hands against the warm skin behind her knees, were somehow a transgression.

He wished he could be more delicate. But he smelled gasoline, and he knew it wasn't safe to leave her here.

Finally he heard the sound of voices, as guests began to run around the side of the house, alerted by Trent. Dr. Marchant was at the front, racing toward them as if he were forty instead of seventy. Susannah was right behind him, her green dress floating around her trim legs.

"Please," the woman in his arms murmured again. She looked at him, the expression in her blue eyes lost and bewildered. He wondered if she might be on drugs. Hitting her head on the windshield might account for this unfocused, glazed look, but it couldn't explain the crazy driving.

"Please, put me down. Susannah… The wedding…"

Chase's arms tightened instinctively, and he froze in his tracks. She whimpered, and he realized he might be hurting her. "Say that again?"

"The wedding. I have to stop it."

* * * * *

Be sure to look for TEXAS BABY,
available September 11, 2007,
as well as other fantastic Superromance titles
available in September.

Welcome to Cowboy Country...

TEXAS BABY

by *Kathleen O'Brien*

#1441

Chase Clayton doesn't know what to think.
A beautiful stranger has just crashed his
engagement party, demanding that he not
marry because she's pregnant with his baby.
But the kicker is—he's never seen her before.

Look for TEXAS BABY and other fantastic
Superromance titles on sale September 2007.

Available wherever books are sold.

The latest novel in The Lakeshore Chronicles
by *New York Times* bestselling author

SUSAN WIGGS

From the award-winning author of *Summer at Willow Lake*
comes an unforgettable story of a woman's emotional journey
from the heartache of the past to hope for the future.

With her daughter grown and flown, Nina Romano is ready to
embark on a new adventure. She's waited a long time for dating,
travel and chasing dreams. But just as she's beginning to enjoy
being on her own, she finds herself falling for Greg Bellamy,
owner of the charming Inn at Willow Lake and a single father
with two kids of his own.

DOCKSIDE

"The perfect summer read." —Debbie Macomber

*Available the first week of August 2007
wherever paperbacks are sold!*

REQUEST YOUR FREE BOOKS!

2 FREE NOVELS PLUS 2 FREE GIFTS!

SPECIAL EDITION®

Life, Love and Family!

YES! Please send me 2 FREE Silhouette Special Edition® novels and my 2 FREE gifts. After receiving them, if I don't wish to receive any more books, I can return the shipping statement marked "cancel." If I don't cancel, I will receive 6 brand-new novels every month and be billed just $4.24 per book in the U.S., or $4.99 per book in Canada, plus 25¢ shipping and handling per book and applicable taxes, if any*. That's a savings of at least 15% off the cover price! I understand that accepting the 2 free books and gifts places me under no obligation to buy anything. I can always return a shipment and cancel at any time. Even if I never buy another book from Silhouette, the two free books and gifts are mine to keep forever.

235 SDN EEYU   335 SDN EEY6

Name	(PLEASE PRINT)	
Address		Apt.
City	State/Prov.	Zip/Postal Code

Signature (if under 18, a parent or guardian must sign)

Mail to the Silhouette Reader Service™:
IN U.S.A.: P.O. Box 1867, Buffalo, NY 14240-1867
IN CANADA: P.O. Box 609, Fort Erie, Ontario L2A 5X3

Not valid to current Silhouette Special Edition subscribers.

Want to try two free books from another line?
Call 1-800-873-8635 or visit www.morefreebooks.com.

* Terms and prices subject to change without notice. NY residents add applicable sales tax. Canadian residents will be charged applicable provincial taxes and GST. This offer is limited to one order per household. All orders subject to approval. Credit or debit balances in a customer's account(s) may be offset by any other outstanding balance owed by or to the customer. Please allow 4 to 6 weeks for delivery.

Your Privacy: Silhouette is committed to protecting your privacy. Our Privacy Policy is available online at www.eHarlequin.com or upon request from the Reader Service. From time to time we make our lists of customers available to reputable firms who may have a product or service of interest to you. If you would prefer we not share your name and address, please check here. ☐

SSE07

ATHENA FORCE

Heart-pounding romance and thrilling adventure.

Professional negotiator Lindsey Novak is faced with her biggest challenge—to buy back Teal Arnett, a young woman with unique powers. In the process Lindsey uncovers a devastating plot that involves scientists from around the globe, and all of them lead to one woman who is bent on destroying Athena Academy…at any cost.

LOOK FOR

THE GOOD THIEF

by Judith Leon

Available September wherever you buy books.

Bailey DelMonico has finally
gotten her life on track, and is
passionate about her recent career
change. Nothing will stand in the way
of her becoming a doctor...that is,
until she's paired with the sharp-tongued
Dr. Ivan Munro.

Watch the sparks fly in

Doctor in
the House

by *USA TODAY* Bestselling Author

Marie Ferrarella

Available September 2007

Intrigued? Read more at
TheNextNovel.com

HARLEQUIN®

N_ext™

HN88141